"Are you   d? You need to tell me if that is true."

"No. I..." She trailed off.

Roman studied her more carefully. "You what? You're sick? Tired? Running the shelter and the salon is too much?"

"All of those things." She held out whatever it was that had been grasped in her hand. It looked like some sort of white pen or plastic piece. "All of those things, and pregnant."

Roman realized it was a pregnancy test in her hand just as she said the words. Now it was his turn for the world to spin slightly.

"Pregnant?"

"Yeah, about eight weeks if I'm not mistaken."

"Okay, now we're definitely getting you to a hospital. You need to be checked out."

She looked over at him, a little surprised. "Aren't you going to ask me if it's yours?"

"You said eight weeks. I'm pretty sure that makes it mine."

CEASE FIRE

USA TODAY **Bestselling Author**

JANIE CROUCH

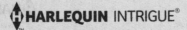

HARLEQUIN INTRIGUE®

This book is dedicated to Rob, who married my friend M. I despaired she would never entrust her heart to someone again, but your patience and unfailing love convinced her. I know you will stand by her side no matter what. You are everything I would've picked for her and more.

ISBN-13: 978-1-335-63924-0

Cease Fire

Copyright © 2018 by Janie Crouch

Recycling programs for this product may not exist in your area.

Printed in U.S.A.

www.Harlequin.com

Janie Crouch has loved to read romance her whole life. This *USA TODAY* bestselling author cut her teeth on Harlequin Romance novels as a preteen, then moved on to a passion for romantic suspense as an adult. Janie lives with her husband and four children overseas. She enjoys traveling, long-distance running, movie watching, knitting and adventure/obstacle racing. You can find out more about her at janiecrouch.com.

Books by Janie Crouch

Harlequin Intrigue

Omega Sector: Under Siege

Daddy Defender
Protector's Instinct
Cease Fire

Omega Sector: Critical Response

Special Forces Savior
Fully Committed
Armored Attraction
Man of Action
Overwhelming Force
Battle Tested

Omega Sector

Infiltration
Countermeasures
Untraceable
Leverage

Primal Instinct

Visit the Author Profile page at Harlequin.com.

CAST OF CHARACTERS

Roman Weber—Omega Critical Response SWAT team member. Recuperating from an explosion that nearly killed him two months ago.

Keira Spencer—Hairdresser who runs a secret women's shelter.

Andrea Gordon Han—Omega Sector behavioral analyst. Longtime friend of Keira's.

Damien Freihof—Terrorist mastermind. Determined to bring down Omega Sector piece by piece by doing what they did to him: destroying their loved ones.

Mr. "Fawkes"—Omega Sector traitor providing inside information to Freihof.

Steve Drackett—Director of the Omega Sector Critical Response Division.

Grace Parker—Omega Sector psychiatrist.

Saul Poniard—New Omega Sector agent desperate to be part of the SWAT team.

Maureen Weber Donovan—Roman's mother.

Annabel Jenkins—Keira's employee and resident at the women's shelter.

Heather McMurray—Resident at the women's shelter with her infant daughter, Rachel.

Jonathan Cunningham—Keira's ex-husband.

Bridgette Cunningham—Keira's former mother-in-law.

Omega Sector—A multiorganizational law enforcement task force made up of the best agents the country has to offer.

Prologue

If you wanted someone killed right, you had to do it yourself.

He should stitch that on a pillow. Damien Freihof smiled as he watched guests enter the church.

He knew from "Mr. Fawkes," his mole inside Omega Sector, that the church had already been swept for explosives and there were guards posted at all the doors. No one without an invitation, and a facial scan to prove their ID, was getting into the building.

It was at least nice to see the law enforcement agency was taking him seriously.

But Damien wasn't crashing the wedding today. Even though it was Brandon Han and Andrea Gordon's, both of whom Damien knew personally. They'd all come so close to dying with each other last year—didn't that bring people closer together?

Damien wasn't at all surprised they were getting married today, just a year later, after the way

Brandon had fought to free Andrea. It had been remarkable, really; the other man's passion—utter determination—to save her.

He'd saved her that day, but in the end it wouldn't be enough. Thanks to Mr. Fawkes's plan, they would all die. Every single member of Omega Sector's critical response team.

But that was for later. Not today.

Today, Damien was just here to look around. To prove to himself how close he could get without anyone realizing who he was. Snap a few pictures.

Particularly of the woman he planned to kill within the next few weeks.

He'd already picked her out. Knew who would die. He hadn't yet decided exactly when or how, but he knew it would be with much fanfare and would definitely garner the attention of those working at Omega.

They had to pay—had to pay for what they'd done to him and his precious Natalie.

Damien's more subtle approach at revenge—convincing others to stalk and kill the people beloved by Omega Sector—hadn't been enough. Yes, one Omega Sector agent had been killed and another put in a coma, but there should've been much more bloodshed by now. Much more grieving.

But Damien had left the killing to others and they had not been able to live up to their commit-

ment. He wouldn't make that mistake this time. Now he would take matters into his own hands.

But not just yet.

Damien was nothing if not a patient man. It had been a while since he'd last struck and it would be a while before he struck again. Just enough time for the law enforcement agents to wonder if he was still here or if he was gone for good.

He hadn't gone anywhere.

And soon, while their defenses were down, he would strike again. Strike at the very heart of them.

Everyone might survive the wedding today.

But they wouldn't survive much longer.

Chapter One

Everyone wore their sidearm to the wedding.

Given that at the last wedding, two months ago, a maniac had burst in and tried to kill the wedding party, firearms were understandable.

Every member of the elite law enforcement task force known as Omega Sector remained determined not to be caught unawares again.

The psychopath at the last wedding had been arrested, and fortunately, no one had been hurt. But everyone knew that as long as Damien Freihof, the mastermind behind the recent attacks against Omega, remained at large, none of them would be safe.

So every agent at Brandon Han and Andrea Gordon's wedding had some sort of holster. Waist, shoulder or ankle for most. A few of the female agents probably had weapons strapped to their thighs or in their evening clutch bags. None of the sidearms were noticeable, but they were there.

Roman Weber had one at both his waist and his

ankle. And there was no way he was letting his guard down tonight.

Thanks to Damien Freihof, Roman hadn't even been able to attend the last Omega Sector wedding. He'd been too busy coming out of a coma from an explosion Freihof had carefully planned. Another Omega Sector agent had been killed. If Roman had been two feet closer to the blast, he would've been killed, too.

So no, Roman wasn't interested in laughing and drinking and dancing, even if many of his closest friends were in the room. Instead, he kept finding his eyes drawn to the multiple entrances to the ballroom of the ski resort here in Colorado Springs, where the reception was being held.

Two main doors leading into the resort, three separate kitchen entrances, and a set of double doors heading out to a terrace. Freihof could attempt to make his way through any of them.

He was around. Roman hadn't seen the man anywhere, but knew in his gut that Freihof was nearby today. The man was so good at disguise it was possible he already waited here inside the room, although Roman didn't think so. There were too many trained agents looking for Freihof for him to risk it.

The guy was a psycho, but he wasn't stupid.

Still, Roman walked over to the shadows closer to the main doors. Just in case.

"See anything suspicious?"

Roman knew Steve Drackett, director of Omega Sector's Critical Response Division, was present before he spoke. Grace Parker, Omega's head psychiatrist, stood beside him.

"No. But it doesn't hurt to keep looking."

Steve nodded. "Damn right about that."

Something inside Roman eased slightly. His boss didn't think he was paranoid. Didn't think searching for Freihof in the shadows of a wedding was being overly cautious.

Steve slapped Roman on the shoulder. "But you do know that watching for Freihof isn't solely your responsibility."

"Maybe not. But it's definitely something I take personally."

Grace smiled at him, tucking a strand of her silver hair behind her ear. "If you didn't take it personally, given what happened, I'd be a lot more concerned."

Roman had spent a lot of time talking to Grace over the past few weeks. The older woman would ultimately be the one who cleared him for active duty once he was cleared physically.

The required sessions with her had been pretty agonizing at first. Roman wasn't a sit-around-and-get-in-touch-with-his-feelings sort of guy. But Grace had made him feel comfortable. She had an air about her that never judged or condescended.

She'd helped him realize how damn pissed off he was that he'd almost died. That Damien Freihof had almost killed him. That it was only sheer blind luck Roman was alive today.

And that all those feelings were normal.

"Am I acting crazy, Doc?"

Grace gave a delicate shrug. "You're acting aware and vigilant. Again, nothing wrong with that."

"I just want to catch this son of a bitch." Roman gritted his teeth just thinking about Freihof.

Steve squeezed his shoulder. "Your medical doctor said you would be clear for active duty next week."

Roman noticed Steve didn't say anything about Grace clearing him mentally. His behavior here tonight wasn't helping. He all but itched with the desire to get back out with his SWAT team on active missions. Desk work was killing him one minute at a time. But active duty was a no-go until he was cleared by both the Omega physician and the psychiatrist.

"Okay, I've got a beautiful family who need my attention." Steve grinned as he looked to where his new wife held their two-week-old son at one of the tables surrounding the dance floor. "Roman, you let me know if you think something's not right. But on the other hand, you're not the only one on duty tonight. Hell, you're not even on duty at all."

Roman and Grace watched Steve walk across the room to his family. Neither of them said anything right away. Roman was going to try to outwait the older woman, but knew that she would win that battle. The psychiatrist had much more practice at the waiting-out-silence game.

"I noticed Steve said that I'd be physically cleared for active duty next week, but he didn't say anything about being cleared by you," Roman finally said, not looking at Grace.

"Do you think you're ready for duty, mentally? Emotionally?" she asked.

"I know that sitting at a desk is doing more harm to my mental health than being active and back out with the team would do."

"And is that what you think I should say in my report?" Grace raised one eyebrow.

Roman had long since learned that almost every statement he gave to Grace would result in another question from her. It didn't bother him anymore. He knew it was just her way of getting him to think through answers for himself.

Grace Parker was a brilliant psychiatrist. She worked with all sorts of people at Omega Sector: agents, victims, and had even acted as the SWAT team's medical doctor in a few emergency situations. If she wasn't twenty or so years older than his own thirty-one, he might have made a move on her long before now. Not that she would've taken him up on the offer.

"You want *me* to say whether I think I'm ready or not," Roman said.

"Ultimately, that's what really matters, isn't it?"

"Not on the piece of paper, it's not. Only your opinion matters, not mine." Roman trusted Grace to give an honest judgment and not hold him back if she thought he was fit for duty.

But damn it, he wanted so badly to be back out in the field he could practically taste it.

"Do you think that I think you're ready?" she asked, turning toward him.

"I would hope so."

"Do you think I think you think I think you're ready?"

Roman tried to wrap his brain around that statement, until he realized Grace was grinning.

"Now you're just messing with me," he said, shaking his head.

Her soft laughter rang out. "Guilty."

Roman smiled now, too, the tension broken. "That's not very nice, you know."

"If it helps, I wouldn't tease you about it if I didn't think you were prepared to join the team in active missions." Grace said.

"Really?" Roman turned to face her more fully.

"Steve didn't mention me clearing you for duty, because I cleared you over a month ago."

She smiled at him. "Mentally, I think you've been ready for a long time. You just needed to give your body some time to rebuild and restrengthen."

"So I'm cleared?" Roman felt tension he'd held for weeks melt off him.

"Yep. As soon as your physician says so."

"You don't think it's a little odd that I'm wearing two weapons here tonight, and wandering from shadow to shadow to make sure Damien Freihof isn't somewhere in the building?"

Grace shook her head. "I'll admit it might be a little bit hyperdiligent. But I promise you, you are not the only person here with two weapons. And you are not the only person here searching the shadows every few minutes. Including the groom."

Roman looked around the room. Grace was probably right. He'd been so caught up in his own need to be sedulous that he hadn't realized there were a dozen others being just as watchful.

"Now, believe it or not, I actually have a date to get back to." Grace smiled again, tilting her head toward a man in his early sixties sitting at a table nearby. Grace's husband had died a few years before and Roman was glad she was seeing someone socially.

"Thank you, Grace. Sometimes it's hard to stay centered."

"That's what I'm here for. That's what we're

all here for. For each other. You've got to remember you're not in this alone. I think that is what Damien Freihof most wants to do—isolate us and fracture us. It's important that we don't let that happen."

Roman nodded. "You're right. I'll try to relax, at least a little bit tonight."

"Aren't your mother and stepfather here? Do you want to spend some time with them?"

Roman refrained from rolling his eyes. Barely. "No, I'd rather sit here and look for invisible bad guys than go hang with my mom and Maxwell, and listen to all the reasons why I should be rubbing elbows with the bigwigs in the room."

Grace laughed. "Well, the state political VIPs are definitely here en masse. And I know you've said your mom would much rather you had gone into politics than be a member of the Omega SWAT team."

"Whether I wanted to or not."

Grace shrugged. "Regardless, they are family. Don't cut them out."

"Trust me, I couldn't cut them out if I wanted to. If you see my mom, don't tell her where I am."

Grace grinned again. "Will do. And Roman, it's a wedding. It's okay to have fun, maybe talk to a girl—like that gorgeous one you've been checking out all night whenever you let your guard ease enough to think about something other than Freihof."

Roman knew exactly who she meant. Keira Spencer. The raven-haired, curvy, petite bridesmaid. One of the bride's friends from high school or something. His attention had been drawn to her tonight like it had at the last few social functions he'd seen her at, as friends of Brandon and Andrea. He would've asked her out long before now if his plans hadn't been waylaid by the whole coma thing.

His eyes left the shadows and sought out the dark-haired beauty now. Like him, she was standing mostly away from the action of the wedding, although he doubted it was for the same reason.

"Exactly," Grace said, touching Roman gently on his arm. "Freihof wants all our attention to be on him, not on living our lives. Let's not give him that satisfaction."

With that she gave him one more smile and made her way back to her date, who politely stood and held out her chair as she sat down, smiling brightly at her as he did so. Roman already liked this guy.

Grace was right. This was a wedding, and it was already midway through the reception. Armed guards stood outside every door. The entire site had been swept extensively for explosives. Trouble in the form of Damien Freihof wasn't making its way in here tonight.

Plus, as Grace had pointed out, they weren't here to focus on the criminal mastermind, they were here to celebrate Brandon and Andrea, two of their own.

Roman didn't know either of them well, but what he did know he liked and respected.

Brandon Han was generally regarded as one of the most intelligent men in the entire country, and his family was an important part of the state government, so this wedding was a grand event. An interesting blend of watchful law enforcement, merry partygoers and political personages networking in a neutral, friendly setting.

The last, Roman knew, included his mother and stepfather. He had no doubt his mom was searching for him, to encourage him to network likewise.

She still hadn't quite embraced the concept that Roman had chosen law enforcement as his means of contributing to society, rather than politics, like his late father.

Roman got a beer from the bar and headed back to the shadows, although this time to avoid trouble rather than search for it.

He wasn't alone for long.

"You've got that 'oh hell, it's another wedding' look on your face."

Roman glanced at the man who had made his way to his side. Damn it, what was his name? Sam Poniard or something. The guy wanted to be SWAT, but for whatever reason hadn't been accepted into the training program.

He shouldn't take it personally. Most people who applied didn't get accepted.

"No kidding." Roman gave a smile to the other man. "Seems like agents around here are falling like flies. You're Sam, right?"

"Saul."

"Saul, that's right. Saul Poniard. Sorry, man. I blame the coma."

Roman could tell he'd offended Saul, but the other man still gave a slight smile. "I guess almost getting blown up is certain to affect your memory."

Roman doubted he would've remembered the other guy's name anyway, but didn't say so. He would be sure to remember it now.

"How's it going for you? Enjoying the party?"

Saul nodded. "Yeah. Not usually my thing, but I thought I would stop in and say hello. Thought it might get me some points."

"Points for what?"

"I'm thinking about reapplying for SWAT."

Roman grimaced. That's why Saul was over here talking to him. He was campaigning. Of course, Roman had zero to do with who got initially accepted into the training program. The leaders might ask the team's opinion before bringing someone on in the final stages, to make sure he or she was a good fit, but not at the beginning.

"Well, good luck with that." Saul appeared fit and strong enough to be in the program. But for whatever reason, he was being overlooked. Roman trusted the people making those choices, Steve Drackett being one of them.

"Maybe we could work out sometime. Spar or something."

"Uh, yeah. Sure, no problem." At least Poniard wasn't asking for a letter of reference or anything. "Hopefully, I'll be cleared for active duty next week. But I'd be happy to do some lighter stuff with you until then."

"That would be awesome. Thanks. Are you hanging back in the shadows looking for Freihof? I've been doing the same thing."

Maybe Poniard would make a better SWAT member than leadership was giving him credit for.

"Yeah. I have to admit I am. Although Steve Drackett was over here a minute ago reminding me that it's okay to relax. That there are other people on guard here."

And Steve and Grace both were right. Roman needed to not let Freihof steal any more of his life. His eyes flew back to Keira, who'd made her way onto the dance floor with the bride and the groom's sisters.

Keira was a much better place to center his attention, rather than searching for an enemy who wasn't here, or avoiding family who wanted what he didn't.

"Yeah, that's true," Saul said. "But I understand. SWAT has to be diligent."

Roman clapped the other man on the shoulder and gave him a smile. "How about if you help us be diligent tonight? Just keep an eye out."

Saul nodded enthusiastically. "Yeah, will do."

Roman excused himself. His mother was moving in his general direction and he had to make sure she didn't catch him. He didn't want a scene tonight.

Roman smiled and took another sip of his beer as he moved away. He loved his mother, even though Maureen Weber Donovan tended to be a little conceited. He knew she loved him and fiercely guarded the family name. She'd remarried after Roman's father, a member of the Colorado General Assembly, had died fifteen years ago, and had never stopped encouraging her children to continue their father's political legacy.

Whether they'd wanted to or not.

Not that Roman wasn't ever going into politics. He just wanted to do it on his own terms, not on his mother's. He wanted to make a difference in the system, and his time at Omega Sector continued to help him understand where the system worked and where it needed fixing.

Roman rubbed a hand over his face and sat down at a table that had been vacated by people out on the dance floor, still glancing around the shadows, looking for danger. A couple months ago he would've been out on the floor with them. Could've kept a watchful eye out while having fun at the same time. He was known as the jokester on the SWAT team. The one with a witty comeback and always ready for a good time, taking nothing too seriously.

Or had been.

He wasn't trying to go back to that persona. He'd been changed at some very basic level by his near-death experience and would never be that same person again.

And although he had no desire to talk politics tonight at his friend's wedding, he could see that perhaps he might be moving in that direction sooner rather than later. Not because he was afraid of death or wanted to get out of the SWAT team, but because now more than ever he realized how short life really was.

Maybe it was just time for him to grow up. Maybe all these changes would've come about regardless. All Roman knew was that he couldn't go back to who he'd been before he'd almost died. Didn't want to go back to who he was formerly.

But before he could move forward with his life, they were going to have to catch Damien Freihof. Although Roman had to make peace that it wasn't going to happen tonight.

Keira had taken herself back off the dance floor and was standing over in the shadows at the side of the room. Roman stood. He was finished staying away from her.

Finished letting Damien Freihof determine every decision he made.

At least for now.

Chapter Two

"How do I know the bride? Oh, we used to be strippers together back in the day."

Keira hadn't actually used that statement as the answer to the question she'd been asked a few times, but that didn't mean it wasn't the truth.

But Andrea, the bride and one of Keira's closest friends, hadn't disclosed her previous line of work, so Keira wouldn't, either.

Although Keira didn't care who knew she was once an exotic dancer. She wasn't ashamed of it. She had clawed her way out of a hell most people would never even conceive, and she wouldn't apologize for how she'd survived. Dancing had been part of that.

But if the bride wanted to keep her past private, that was certainly her prerogative. Keira wouldn't reveal the information, either.

"Hey there, beautiful. You doing okay?"

The bride had somehow sneaked up on Keira

right as she'd been thinking about her. Their arms wrapped around each other.

"Yes! What are you doing over here with me? Brandon's going to be looking for you."

Andrea smiled, her straight blond hair in stark contrast to Keira's riotous dark curls. "He's watching me, I can feel it. I'm not sure where he is exactly, but I can guarantee he knows where I am."

Keira laughed. "If he wasn't so crazy in love with you, that would be sort of stalkerish. But I know what you mean."

Andrea's smile, as always, was soft and sweet. She was never going to be someone who wanted to draw attention to herself if she had other options. That had been true even back in their dancing days. Keira still didn't know how Andrea had managed to survive it.

Except that Andrea was a survivor.

Ultimately, that had drawn Keira and Andrea together, the two of them so opposite in personality, looks and temperament. Survivor had recognized survivor.

"I love you, Andrea." Keira brought her friend in for another hug. "And I'm so excited for you here on your beautiful day, and for the stalker standing over there with some friends, looking at you with adoration in his eyes."

"Do you really think this turned out okay?" Doubt tinged Andrea's voice. "This wedding was so much bigger than I wanted. This reception so elaborate. It's just that Brandon's family is involved with politics and business. They wanted to do the whole big thing."

"It's perfect. The wedding was beautiful, everyone is having a good time at the reception and you're handling it all like a champ."

Andrea didn't have her own family—her parents had died when she was young, and the people who'd raised her afterwards had made her home life so bad that she'd run away as a teen rather than stay there—but Keira had to admit the Hans had embraced her with such open arms that she could hardly claim no family anymore. They loved their son and loved their new daughter-in-law.

Proof was in Brandon's sisters making their way over to Andrea a few minutes later and pulling her out on the dance floor.

As they went, a man—the very epitome of tall, dark and handsome—caught Keira's attention from across the room, over near the terrace doors. He was studying her in a way that made her insides begin a slow burn. Keira knew he was an Omega agent, had seen him around at a couple events in the last few months, but didn't know his name. Had been afraid to ask in case she couldn't stop herself from pouncing on him.

Her attention was yanked back by Andrea.

"Come join us!" the bride said over her shoulder, a new sister attached to each arm as they crossed to the dance floor.

"In a few." Keira laughed and waved. She looked over again, but tall, dark and handsome seemed to have moved back into the shadows.

She shrugged, surprised by how disappointed she was to lose that moment with him. She didn't tend to be so romantic as allowing herself to feel heat from just a glance.

Didn't tend to be romantic at all.

But Keira didn't head to the dance floor. Most people had brought a date to dance with. Keira deliberately had not because, as one of the bridesmaids, she wanted to be able to concentrate on Andrea and anything she needed. But mostly because she just didn't date much.

Keira looked around at the large crowd. There seemed to be two types of people populating the wedding. Omega Sector agents, all half mingling, half watching the door for any sign of that maniac who had almost killed both Andrea and Brandon last year. They were intelligent, they were armed and they were ready.

And they weren't even the most dangerous people in the room. That was the other part of the crowd.

The wealthy. The privileged. The elite.

Those people scared Keira much more than someone with a gun did.

They shook hands and slapped backs, then stuck proverbial knives in those very same backs as soon as it served their best interests. The room was filled with men and women who aspired to be congressmen, governors, maybe even more. Those who desired to start, run and sell multimillion dollar corporations.

And they had the power—or the family with power—to back up those goals.

She knew these types of people, knew what they could do to someone. Had been married to a member of a family like the ones here. One who had powerful political aspirations.

Six years ago, she had fled this state a broken person. Not much more than a child. She had bought her freedom from the upper echelon with her own blood, always afraid the man who'd broken her would wield his wealth and power to find her again.

His family wasn't here tonight; Keira had made sure that would be the case long before this day came. She'd asked Brandon, not Andrea, if the Cunningham family of Denver would be attending the wedding. Brandon hadn't thought so and had double-checked, since his parents—who were paying for the wedding—were inviting some business and political associates he didn't know well.

He was soon able to assure her there would be no Cunninghams in attendance.

Keira had expected Brandon to press for details, but he hadn't. Just gave her that look that said he'd probably already figured out 90 percent of the situation in that huge brain of his, and moved on to other questions, about wedding bands and cake flavors.

Keira had been relieved she wouldn't have to miss one of her closest friends' weddings. But she would have to avoid Jonathan Cunningham and his family.

There weren't many things Keira was afraid of in this world. But a family willing to use its wealth and power to hide the hideous sins of its son?

Let's just say she was never getting involved with anyone from a wealthy and powerful family again.

Not that she had much interest in attaching herself to anyone on a permanent basis. When the bouquet was tossed in a little bit, Keira would definitely not be part of the group trying to catch it. She'd already lived through her own hell of a marriage once. That was plenty for one lifetime.

Andrea waved to her from the dance floor and Keira made her way out there. No more boo-hooing over the past. Keira had survived. She would always survive.

Breathe in, breathe out, move on.

Keira joined the group out on the floor, jumping and waving their hands over their heads to an upbeat song. Andrea was positively glowing. Keira was so glad her friend had found her knight in shining armor.

Keira didn't need one. She preferred to fight her own battles and had now finally gotten herself situated to help others who needed assistance.

Help people like the scared, broken girl she'd once been.

After a few more dances, things began to wind down. The speeches were given, the cake cut, the music became slower. She noticed some women sliding their high heels off to give their feet a rest. Keira didn't need to, one of the perks of her ex-occupation.

She grinned to herself from the edge of the ballroom, where she stood in the shadows. Her three-inch heels were nothing compared to most of the shoes she'd danced in at the club. Plus they made her seem not quite so pitifully short.

"I have to admit, you look like someone very pleased with herself."

The deep voice startled her and she glanced to her side.

Wow. Tall, dark and handsome had decided to join her in the shadows.

"Sorry, didn't mean to spook you." His smile was so charming she couldn't help but smile back.

"I just didn't think anyone was hiding here but me. At least on this side of the room."

"Are you hiding?"

Keira shrugged a shoulder exposed by her strapless dress. "Only because I'm afraid Andrea's going to throw the bouquet in a minute."

He chuckled. "You gathering your strength to wipe out the competition?"

Keira raised an eyebrow. "Are you kidding? Look at them." She waved her arm toward some of the single women at the tables in the middle of the room. "I don't need to gather my strength to take them out."

"I stand corrected." He laughed softly again, the sound doing things to Keira's insides she hadn't felt in a long while.

"But no, I'm over here because I don't want anyone to notice when I don't join in the tradition of tackling poor, defenseless flowers."

"I thought all single women wanted to catch the bouquet."

She turned completely toward him so she could give him the full weight of her opinion of that asinine statement.

But instead just got caught up in the ridiculous blue of his eyes, coupled with his brown hair. She literally felt her breath catch at the spark between them.

So much for not being romantic.

He felt it, too. She could tell by the way he eased closer. "I stand corrected again. Not every woman wants to make a flying tackle for the bouquet. I'm Roman Weber. I work with Brandon and Andrea at Omega."

"Nice to meet you, Roman Weber. I'm Keira Spencer, old friend of the bride."

"I've seen you around."

Yeah, she'd seen him, too, since she'd moved to Colorado Springs six months ago. But she'd never had a chance to talk to him before now. Or really, Keira hadn't pushed it. Had deliberately not let herself be pulled in by the instant attraction between the two of them.

With him standing beside her, she couldn't help but be pulled in by it now.

"Dance with me?" He tilted his head down near her ear and whispered the words softly. The music was slow. Sultry even. Definitely not helping her resist this attraction pooling in her.

"I'm trying to stay out of the lights on the dance floor, remember?" But she knew if he led her out there she would definitely not resist.

She felt his arm slide low around her waist. "Not out there," he whispered. "Right here."

He pulled her into him and began to gently sway with the music. His other hand found hers and brought it up against his chest, keeping their fingers entwined.

Even with her heels she barely came up to his chin. She knew this sort of closeness should make her feel uncomfortable, and waited for that tinge of panic to assail her.

It never came.

One song led into a second as they moved slowly together, in perfect rhythm.

"Why are you hiding in the shadows, Roman Weber?" Keira asked as the second slow song ended and the band took a break for the bouquet and garter toss.

"I'm dancing in the shadows with a gorgeous woman," Roman replied.

"Not hiding from the garter?"

He smiled. And still hadn't slipped his arm from her waist or released her hand from his chest.

"No. Although I will admit, shamefully, since I'm a grown man, that I'm trying to avoid my mother and her nagging agenda at events like this."

Keira smiled. "Mom's not a big fan of you working at Omega Sector?"

"Oh yes, believe me, she is not happy about my chosen profession."

She couldn't blame a mother for being concerned about her son's well-being. Keira could feel the muscles of the chest beneath her fingers, the light balance he had on his feet. Roman was definitely an active agent. Probably regularly in the line of fire. A mother could be forgiven for nagging about that.

"I understand the hiding. Even if I wasn't trying to avoid the bouquet, I generally avoid crowds like this."

He eased back so they could see each other's eyes. "Law enforcement agents?"

"No." She shook her head, smiling. "The other ones. Rich and privileged, with an agenda of their own."

Roman studied her for a long moment in a way she didn't really understand.

"What?" she finally asked.

"Nothing." His gaze turn into something softer, more inviting. "You're trying to get away from these people. I'm trying to get away from these people. What do you say we just get out of here together, right now? I have a suite upstairs."

She raised an eyebrow.

"It can just be for more dancing. I promise." That smile again that took her breath away. "All I'm trying to do is save you from the plant-damaging violence of the bouquet toss. Although I agree, you could definitely take out most of the women here."

Despite what some people might think of her because of her past profession, giving in to an instant attraction wasn't Keira's normal way of doing things. Letting a man get close to her was difficult. Hell, given her previous marriage, even being attracted to someone was a novelty.

But the attraction between her and Roman Weber was something fierce. She couldn't deny it even if she wanted to.

And she didn't want to.

For the first time in her life, Keira threw caution to the wind. "What if I'm interested in more than just dancing up in your suite?"

His grinned widened. "Then I would ask why the heck we're still here talking about it."

He let go of her waist and pulled her to the door.

Chapter Three

They didn't leave the suite for the next day and a half.

They hardly left the bed except to grab what they ordered from room service.

Keira couldn't stop smiling. She came back out of the bathroom midday Monday after brushing her teeth and attempting to do something with her hair, hardly recognizing the woman she'd seen in the mirror.

Spending the weekend in bed with a man she hardly knew really wasn't part of her MO. She may have been an exotic dancer, but that hadn't meant she'd allowed men close to her. As a matter of fact, stripping had been the furthest thing from intimacy for her.

While onstage, she'd known exactly what moves to do to make the most money and gather the most attention. And even offstage she'd always been confident and capable, her thriving salon business now proof of that.

But when it came to intimacy with a man, Keira was much more wary. Her confidence much lower. She could thank Jonathan Cunningham for that. After her disastrous sham of a marriage, she'd been afraid to get close to anyone.

She could count on two fingers the number of relationships she'd had since her divorce six years ago. And that was including whatever was going on with Roman right now.

He'd already taken her phone's calendar and scheduled her to have dinner with him every night this week, so evidently he planned on them seeing each other again after they left here.

And she couldn't stop smiling. Not her fake-but-sparkling stage smile, but her legit, bubbling-from-somewhere-deep-inside smile.

"I like that look on you," he said, as she crossed to him with the sheet wrapped around her.

"Sheets are all the rage this season." She twirled as if she was on a runway, then let out a yelp as he grabbed the sheet and pulled it off her.

"That's even better," he murmured, using the sheet still wrapped around her hips to pull her closer. His lips melded to hers and she melted into him.

"You know we have to leave this room some-time," she finally said against his mouth.

"How about if I quit my job at Omega and you close the salon?"

She giggled. "I'm pretty sure they'd kick us out of here soon, when we run out of money."

"Argh. Damn consumerism in the US."

His phone buzzed again on the nightstand. Hers had been doing the same thing for the last few hours.

The real world was calling.

It was late Monday afternoon. The salon was closed on Sundays and Mondays, so it had worked out fine to be here with Roman. But she had paperwork to do and the salon involved much more than just cutting and styling hair.

But she hadn't explained any of that to Roman yet. Even though he was law enforcement, she still wasn't completely comfortable sharing the Fresh Starts salon's true purpose. Those secrets weren't fully hers to tell.

"I've got to get back to the salon."

"I thought it wasn't open today."

"It's not. But paperwork and shipments and handling stuff all keep going no matter what day it is. The glorious life of a small business owner."

"And I guess I've got to go back to Omega and sit at a desk all day." He gave the most adorable pout, lying there against the pillows.

"Aw." She trailed her fingers down his cheek. "Poor little SWAT team member frustrated by having to use his brain?"

She joked, but the burn scars he had across his

chest and shoulder from his close call with death two months ago were anything but funny.

He spun her around and had her pinned under him in a second flat.

"I'll admit I'm much more prone to action than I am profiling or researching." He bent down to kiss her and shifted his hips so they were more fully pressed up against each other. Keira couldn't stop the moan that escaped her as his lips worked their way across her jaw and down her neck.

His phone rang again. This time the music from the movie *Jaws*. Keira laughed. It wasn't the first time that person had called.

She pushed at his chest to stop his lips from going lower down her shoulder.

"Okay, I've got to know who that is. The *Jaws* theme."

Roman propped himself up on his elbow and rolled his eyes. "My mother."

Keira threw her head back and let out a laugh. Until Roman took advantage of her exposed throat and soon had her gasping for breath.

But when the shark theme came again from his phone five minutes later, Keira knew she had to get him to answer it.

"Roman, it's your mother."

"She'll call back."

"Uh, yeah, in another five minutes. You said

she doesn't like your Omega job. She's worried about you."

After what had happened with that explosion that had almost killed him, Keira didn't blame his mom. She nudged him. "Just answer it so she won't be worried."

He didn't look thrilled, but he did it. Probably because he knew his mother wasn't going to stop calling until she knew he was safe.

"Hello, Mother."

Immediately, Keira could hear his mother talking at a rate and pitch that had to be barely discernible even to Roman. Keira couldn't make out a bit of it and she was only six inches away.

Roman kept the receiver at his ear and bent down to kiss Keira again. A luscious kiss that almost made her forget the other woman on the line. But all too soon, he ended the kiss and pushed back.

"Of course I'm listening."

He winked at Keira and got up from the bed, walking naked across the room toward the window. "I left the wedding early with a friend." He glanced back at Keira and smiled. "Yes, someone I met at the wedding, and that's why I left. Well, met again. We have mutual friends."

Keira didn't think she'd ever get tired of looking at Roman's naked form. Hard to believe those six-pack abs and firm buttocks were what he looked like now, during recovery. Him in top physical form just might kill her.

"Keira Spencer." He waited patiently while his mother said something else. "I tell you what, why don't I check with her and see if she's available to join us all for lunch next Sunday?"

Keira's eyes flew to Roman's. Did he really want her to join his family for lunch? He was smiling reassuringly at her. Maybe this wasn't as big a deal as she thought.

Regardless, she got up while he was finishing with his mom. She needed some sort of fortification right now. Clothes seemed like a good start.

She dressed, glad she had grabbed her change of clothes and toiletries from the hotel room she'd booked but hadn't used. She was putting on some makeup when he finished his conversation and tapped on the door.

"You okay in there?"

She opened it. "Dinner with the family? Does that mean I get to wear your letterman's jacket, too?"

He stole a kiss. "Smart-ass. You don't have to go if you don't want to. Sunday lunches with my family are sort of a networking event. Everybody brings someone if they want. I don't always even go."

Was he backpedaling? Did he not want her

there? She didn't know him well enough to know how to respond. "Oh. Well…"

"I tell you what. Have dinner with me every night this week and then if you still like me, you can come hang with the family. They're pretty overwhelming."

She laughed and shook her head at his crazy proposal. "I can't have dinner with you every night this week. The salon is open late some nights."

"I'll bring takeout."

It was nice to be wanted, and by someone not only so damn attractive, but trustworthy also. He was a friend of Andrea and Brandon's and worked for one of the top law enforcement agencies in the country. Pretty damn trustworthy.

And although they hadn't gotten into each other's financial background in the hours they'd talked in between bouts of lovemaking over the last two days, Keira felt safe in assuming Roman wasn't part of the high society group she'd left behind six years ago. Nobody born with a silver spoon and aspirations of power became a member of SWAT, putting his life in danger every day.

Roman Weber was pretty close to damn well perfect.

He finally wore her down, and she agreed to having dinner with him two nights and the meal with his family on Sunday.

It was crazy and scary and oh-so-exciting.

For the first time in six years, Keira could actually imagine a relationship with someone. Maybe not marriage—she wasn't sure she'd ever be ready for that—but something long term. Permanent.

There were still obstacles, of course, Keira very definitely wasn't naive. One utterly fabulous weekend did not necessarily mean they'd have something going on long term.

But it was a hell of a start.

Chapter Four

When Sunday rolled around and Roman picked her up for the mid-afternoon lunch with his family, Keira was still on cloud nine.

She'd thought that Roman would pull back, try to play it cool this week. To maybe ease out of their meal-with-family plan.

Actually, Keira was surprised she hadn't pulled back herself. It was all a little scary.

And although they'd toned it down a little physically, both of them wanting to reset and ease more gently into whatever was happening between them, she'd seen or talked to Roman every day this week.

She felt like Cinderella waiting for the clock to strike midnight and everything around her to turn into a pumpkin. Things couldn't continue to go as well as they'd been going.

Fresh Starts continued to thrive also. Not just the salon part, although Keira could admit she was damn good at styling hair, but its fuller purpose: providing women who had nowhere else to go a shelter. Apartments where they could stay as long as they needed. And then training in cosmetology, so the women had a way of supporting themselves.

Keira had sunk all the money she'd had left of her inheritance—money she'd desperately needed when she was younger, but that her parents had thought they were being so wise in putting into a trust fund untouchable until she was twenty-five—into the shop, the equipment and the building. She owned it all, free and clear. No debt, which allowed all the earnings from the salon to funnel back into the shelter.

And she would use it all to help as many women as possible. Help them get out of abusive or trafficking situations. Help them learn they had other choices, other options, than what they'd grown accustomed to. She had three women living there now.

She still hadn't told Roman about the safeguarding aspect of the salon. It was too soon. That wasn't something you told someone you'd been dating for only a week.

Dating. She grinned at the word.

"What are you smiling about over there?" He reached out and grabbed her hand with one of his, keeping the other firmly on the steering wheel.

"Just at what a difference a week makes. If you

had asked me a little over a week ago what I would be doing this Sunday, I would've put a million dollars on anything but this."

He gave her a crooked grin. "Yeah, this week was pretty unexpected for me also."

"I'm not trying to rush things."

"Me, either. Let's just have this lunch with my parents to get my mom off my case, and then we can take things at our own pace."

"Sounds perfect."

He looked her up and down and wagged an eyebrow. "As long as our own pace means I can take you back to my place tonight."

She ran her hand through his thick brown hair as he drove. "I think that can be arranged. So are we going to your parents' house? Do your brother and sister both come over every week?"

The thought of a mom cooking for her family even though the kids were all out of the house was pretty heartwarming.

"We don't get together every week. Usually it's more like once a month. Daniel is off at college. Angela comes if she can be bothered and sometimes brings her fiancé, Brock."

"I think it's great." For someone with no siblings and dead parents it all sounded sort of lovely.

But a few minutes later, when Roman made a turn into the entrance of the Colorado Springs Country Club, Keira's good feelings started to ebb.

"The country club?" She tried to give a light laugh, but it came out sounding as brittle as she felt.

"Yeah." Roman smiled at her, unaware of her tension. "I guess I should've mentioned that my mother doesn't really cook. All our family dinners or lunches are here."

Keira tried to squash the panic bubbling up through her system.

Just because they were at a country club did not mean that Roman's family was anything like Jonathan's family. A country club membership did not necessarily mean power and privilege. Lots of people were involved in a country club. Regular, happy, kind people who also happened to have money. Or liked to play golf.

The words didn't settle the panic in her system.

Keira remained silent as they drove up to the covered portico of the clubhouse. What could she say without sounding completely ridiculous? That country clubs threw her into a panic because of what had happened to her in her past?

She and Roman hadn't gotten into any of that. It wasn't anything she wanted to talk about. Wasn't anything she'd thought she'd *needed* to talk about.

The valet opened the car door for her and she automatically stepped out, thankful she'd worn a nice knit dress coupled with heeled boots for this *casual* meal she'd thought she'd be attending. What if she had worn jeans? Would they have let her in?

Even Roman coming around the car and putting a hand on the small of her back in a protective gesture couldn't stop her sense of foreboding.

"The most important thing to remember is just not to take my family too seriously." He smiled at her again and still didn't seem to realize how panicked she was, thank goodness. "I surely don't."

Keira didn't answer as she studied the people around her. This country club was no different than the ones she'd gone to in Denver when she'd been married to Jonathan. Everyone was still chatting, shaking hands, slapping backs, congratulating themselves on being masters of their universe. It was a typical Sunday afternoon at a place like this.

Keira knew she was being unreasonable, that it was unfair to judge everyone on the actions of the few, but she couldn't help it. She felt like she was going to throw up. She had to get a grip.

"There you are!" A woman in her midsixties, with perfectly styled brown hair in a bob, rushed over to them. "I thought you said you'd be here at one o'clock."

"I didn't think I needed to bring Keira for mimosas, Mother." Roman leaned down and kissed the woman on her cheek as she offered it up to him. "Family lunch is quite enough."

Roman's hand rubbed circles at the small of Keira's back. "Mother, I'd like for you to meet Keira Spencer. Keira, this is my mother, Maureen Weber Donovan."

Maureen turned to Keira and for just a moment disdain burned in her eyes, before she quickly masked it.

"So glad you could join us so we could get to talk to you today," Maureen said. "Roman doesn't bring many of his girls around to meet us."

The snub that Keira was just one of many, and therefore unimportant, was slight and said so gently it was almost unrecognizable.

Definitely recognizable was that this family obviously had money. It surrounded everything about Maureen, from how she dressed, to her walk, to her scent. It was all expensive and expertly finished.

They walked over to the table where the rest of Roman's family sat, and introductions were made. Maureen introduced her husband, Maxwell Donovan, who was not Roman's father but the man Maureen had married after Roman's father had died fifteen years ago.

Maxwell Donovan was much more interested in the drink in his hand and the football game he had on his smart phone than he was in anything happening at the table.

Roman's sister and her fiancé had also joined

them. They seemed nice enough and by the time everyone had ordered lunch, Keira felt like maybe she had imagined the entire thing with Maureen when they'd first met.

The meal was fine, tasty. Everyone made light, mostly meaningless conversation. Even Maxwell joined in at times, although no one seemed offended when he would jump out of a conversation and back into his game when he felt it necessary. Roman's smile had Keira relaxing and thinking that she'd allowed her paranoia to cloud her judgment earlier.

Which was why she was so unprepared for the attack when it occurred.

Keira couldn't fault Maureen in her timing: she waited for dessert. If she had done it any earlier in the meal it would've just made everything awkward. Instead, she went for the kill in between bites of crème brûlée.

"So you two met at the wedding last week?" Maureen's smile didn't falter at the question.

Roman smiled over at Keira before answering. "Yes, although we had seen each other before the wedding and knew each other through mutual friends. But last week was the first time we truly connected."

Keira appreciated that he was trying to make their relationship sound a little more respectable than how they'd actually got started. Not that she was ashamed of it, but telling his mother the hot details seemed unnecessary.

But Maureen Donovan had plans of her own.

"So I noticed you were one of the bridesmaids. How do you know Andrea?"

"She and I worked together a few years ago."

Maureen looked over at Keira. "Was that before, during or after you were a stripper?"

The words were stated clearly, distinctly enough to make sure not only everyone at their table could hear them, but those guests sitting at the tables surrounding them, as well.

Keira realized she should've expected it. She knew people like this. Knew what they were capable of. And yet she'd let herself be drawn in here thinking that being on Roman's arm could protect her.

She wasn't stupid. She didn't know why she had made such a stupid mistake.

Maureen calmly took the napkin out of her lap and folded it, placing it on the table beside her plate as chaos ensued around her. At the word *stripper*, even Maxwell had turned off his beloved football game. Angela and her fiancé had both gasped and gone wide-eyed, looking back and forth between Roman and Keira.

Roman narrowed his eyes and looked at Maureen. "What are you talking about, Mother? Andrea Gordon Han is an agent at Omega Sector."

Maureen glanced at her son. "But she wasn't always an agent at your beloved law enforcement agency—" her eyes turned back to Keira "—was she?"

Keira refused to allow herself to be browbeaten by this woman. "I can't speak to Andrea's past, but yes, I used to be a stripper. It was quite lucrative, actually."

Keira could feel Roman studying her, but she didn't even look at him. She knew where her enemy was and it was right across the table.

And Maureen wasn't done. "And now you're a hairdresser? Is that correct, dear?"

"Yes, it is." Keira took her napkin and folded it next to her dessert plate just as Maureen had.

"I would imagine that's not quite as lucrative as taking your clothes off—and whatever else you did—for money." Maureen's smile never faltered.

"Mother, that's enough." Roman's voice held a cold anger, but Keira honestly wasn't sure if it was directed toward his mother or toward her.

Maureen strategically knew when not to push. "Of course, dear. I was just pointing out that a new business can be such a drain on the pocketbook. I wasn't sure if Keira maybe had discussed needing assistance from you."

In other words, that Keira was using Roman for his money. Ironically, if she had known Roman and his family had such wealth she would've never gotten involved with him in the first place. She'd thought she'd just been getting involved with a law enforcement agent.

"I can assure you the salon is doing just fine and in no need of financial assistance from your family." Keira stood. "As a matter fact, I would like to thank you for the lovely lunch, but now I should probably be getting back to the salon."

Maureen smiled. "Of course, dear, you should get back to where you belong. A new business owner always wants to be with her business."

A few minutes later, after tense goodbyes, Roman had the car pulled around by the valet and they both slipped inside, the silence between them thick and heavy. Neither of them knew quite what to say. No matter how much Keira wanted it to be different, Maureen's words had hit them both hard.

The drive back from the country club was more of the same. Except for agreeing to go back to the salon rather than his place, there didn't seem to be much to say.

Roman finally spoke as they pulled up. "My mother—"

Keira cut him off. "Your mother is the matriarch of a family with wealth and power. She wants to protect you. And your family name."

Keira was intimately familiar with that sort of

family protection. It had nearly cost her her life six years ago.

"But still, what she said wasn't…" he seemed to struggle to find the correct word "…polite."

Polite. No, talking about someone's tawdry prior profession at a country club wouldn't seem polite to him.

Keira shook her head. "That doesn't mean it wasn't true. I *was* a stripper, Roman. I did take off my clothes for money. I don't apologize for it or try to hide it. And I am a hairdresser now."

"I know that."

They sat there in silence for long minutes, neither of them knowing what to say.

"Look." Keira finally broke the quiet. "We probably jumped into this relationship thing too quickly. Let hormones or lust or whatever get the best of us. Maybe we should just say we had a great week, super fantastic sex, and leave it at that."

Because Keira couldn't get involved with a man from a powerful, well-connected family again. She just didn't have it in her.

Roman looked relieved. "Yeah. Maybe so. Just let it breathe for a while."

But they both knew "letting it breathe" meant letting it go.

Roman opened the car door for her and hugged her before he left. They both mentioned something about getting together sometime in the future. They both didn't mean it. Roman gave her a small smile and wave before driving away.

And right there in the late afternoon, the clock struck midnight and everything around her turned to pumpkins.

Chapter Five

Two Months Later

"Who's up for a beer once we get off?" Liam Goetz asked as the SWAT team was heading back late in the afternoon from a full-day wilderness training course.

The Omega Sector SWAT team wasn't often called in to do wilderness work, but it did happen. Therefore, training happened.

But this just seemed to be another long day in a series of long days for Roman.

"Don't ask Roman, for God's sake," Lillian said, rolling her eyes. "He's cranky. Again. This has something to do with a woman, I'm telling you."

"I'm not cranky," Roman protested, even though he knew it was just going to feed their argument. "And it has nothing to do with a woman. It's just been a long-ass day."

But his team was right; Roman was irritable. He'd been cranky for two months now.

And he knew exactly why he was grumpy, although he'd be damned if he'd admit it to anyone.

"Yeah, you tell him 'em, Roman." Liam nodded supportively. "My wife was pregnant with twins, so I know what cranky looks like. And you're only a little bit like that."

The rest of the team chuckled, even Derek, their leader, so Roman knew he'd been pretty bad. John Cornell and Saul Poniard, two guys not part of the normal SWAT team, were with them—Poniard probably still trying to get bonus points like he had at the wedding—looking both confused and amused at the banter. Cornell studied them all like they were science projects. The guy gave Roman the creeps.

"I'd be irritable, too, if I had almost been blown up," Ashton Fitzgerald, the team's sharpshooter, said. "Oh, wait, I was almost blown up."

Lillian rolled her eyes again. "You found the love of your life in that situation, Fitzy. Weber didn't. So you're not supposed to be cranky."

Fitzgerald held out his hands in mock surrender. "I'm just glad you guys aren't mocking me about being Summer's handyman anymore."

Even Roman had to smile at that. They'd teased Ashton mercilessly over his crush on Summer Worrall and the fact that she'd thought he was her condo building's handyman for the longest time.

"Oh, I'm sure she still thinks you're handy."

Liam wagged his eyebrows. "Just for more than fixing her sink now."

"All right, boys and girls, it looks like nobody is getting a beer tonight," Derek said, breaking in. "We just got a call. Emergency hostage drill at the simulator."

Nobody groaned out loud, but everybody wanted to. Not that they minded being thrown extra training at the end of a long day. They expected that, even welcomed it, to keep the team focused and prepared.

Their apprehension lay with the training center itself. Everyone glanced in Fitzgerald's direction, since he'd been the one almost killed in the very first training op in the simulator months ago.

"Don't look at me. As long as we don't have to wear the suits, I'm all for it," Fitzgerald said.

Derek nodded. "No suits. No suits for the foreseeable future."

The mesh suits, which were supposed to have simulated a gunshot wound by giving the team member a small electric shock, had malfunctioned and shocked Fitzy's body over and over, until the SWAT team had finally cut the power to the whole building and saved his life.

The suits were great in theory, but in practice ended up being a bust.

With rumors that it had been deliberate sabotage.

"The call is one hostage and one perp. Federal office building."

"One bad guy, boss? Seems a little lax, doesn't it?" Lillian asked.

Derek shrugged. "Maybe they're taking pity on us since we've already put in a fifteen-hour day, but somehow I doubt it." The SWAT truck pulled up to the training simulator. "So let's be ready for whatever they're going to throw at us. Poniard, Cornell, you can come in, too, but you'll need to stay back."

John Cornell nodded, but Poniard looked disappointed that he wouldn't be able to be part of the action. The guy definitely wanted to be SWAT.

The multimillion-dollar training simulator was designed to be different every time a team went in. The designers could pull up multiple scenarios and realistic-looking robotic bad guys, who were pretty accurate in terms of their "choices" and actions. Some of the best video game programmers and computer engineers in the world had developed the system. Once they got all the kinks worked out—for example, the suits not accidentally almost killing someone—law enforcement groups from all over the country would come here to train. Omega was very fortunate to have it in their backyard.

The team entered the giant warehouse-type building, into a holding room. There they traded out their real weapons for simulated ones. They weighed about the same and even felt very similar, but shot light beams rather than bullets.

The countdown was given, the door opened and the team walked into a replica of any generic urban area. This time it was a downtown situation, at night, with rain. Actual mist was simmering in the air around them. Darkness surrounded them except for what little light the streetlamps provided.

"Cornell, Poniard, this is as far as you go. Everybody else, keep your eyes peeled," Derek said. "One perp can't be right."

Roman couldn't agree more. The Omega SWAT team got called in for cases bigger than what local PD could handle, or if a situation occurred on federal property.

One bad guy in one office? Omega wouldn't be called in for that, and it didn't do that much good to train for it, either. But they would, regardless.

"Fitzy, Liam, head around back. I'm sure there's some sort of fire escape on a building this old. Lil, find us a completely separate way into the office in case we need it. Roman and I will take the front. Let's use cameras to see what we're dealing with here, and watch your backs."

Everyone took off in their assigned direction. Fitzgerald and Liam were the first to check in.

"We've got a visual on the suspect and the hostage. Hostage is female, according to the dress she's wearing, tied to a chair, and has some sort of sack over her head. Suspect is pacing back and forth," Fitzgerald reported.

"Or pacing as much as a robot can," Liam added.

"Okay, pacing means agitated," Roman commented. "Agitated means unpredictable. And like Derek said, watch for a partner."

Roman and Derek were at the office door, which opened to a hallway. Derek positioned the camera cord under the door; that would allow them to get a visual feed from the room. Roman guarded the hallway to make sure no one would be able to come up on them unawares.

"Okay, confirm that," Derek said, once the camera was in place. "Looks like we don't have anybody else in the front room, either. I can see the suspect pace by."

"Derek, I found a way into the air vent and have a good view of the entire room." Lillian's voice came through very soft in their ears. "Believe it or not, I think this is just a one-person gig. I can take him out without killing him and we can end this right now. Still have time for the beer and more of Roman's crankiness."

Roman rolled his eyes. This was too damn easy. "Maybe they're keeping it simple this time. We're always ready for the big baddies, but sometimes we just come up against a lone wolf."

"Let's hold for five minutes and see what happens," Derek said. "Because this is a damn waste of good beer time if this is all they've got for us."

Five minutes came and passed with nothing but the "hostage taker" continuing to pace.

"Okay, we breach on my mark," Derek finally said. "Lillian, you take the guy out without killing him, everybody else enters to give her any backup she needs."

"Roger that," the team echoed back.

Roman wasn't sure what he was expecting, maybe ninjas falling out of the sky or a bomb under the conference room table.

But nothing like that happened.

Maybe, like he'd told Derek, this was an exercise in restraint, to make sure the team was ready to handle a situation that required less brawn and more finesse.

But it still sucked.

The team entered the office building at the same time Lillian dropped from the air duct. She rolled as she landed, and shot the suspect in the shoulder, causing the simulated gun he held in his hand to fall to the ground.

Within moments the rest of the team had "cuffed" the bad guy so he could do no further harm to anyone.

Mission over.

"Okay," Liam said. "That was almost as relaxing as getting a beer."

Fitzgerald laughed. "Honestly, I thought the floor was going to turn to acid or something."

"My bet was on flesh-eating zombies," Lillian said.

Roman went over and took the sack off the "victim's" head. But where a realistic robot face should've been was some sort of television screen.

With the picture of a woman, also wearing a dress, also tied to a chair, also with a sack over her head.

"What the hell?" Roman said. The rest of the team rushed over.

"So glad you could defeat one single perpetrator."

Curses flooded the training center as the team watched Damien Freihof come into view on the screen.

"You have such a difficult time catching me, I thought we better see if you could catch a single bad guy in the simulator." Freihof smiled for the camera.

"Where is he?" Roman muttered to the team.

"Not here, that's for sure," Lillian returned. "That's a real office, not the simulator."

Freihof's face took up the entire screen once again. "Before we continue, let's make sure we have everybody at Omega on board."

A few seconds later, Roman felt his cell phone buzz in his pocket. He grabbed it, only to see Freihof's picture come up on that screen, too. It looked like the same thing was happening to the rest of the team on their phones.

"I want to apologize to you," Freihof said, looking impossibly genuine. "I've been toying with you, and the people who I've been working with haven't always been successful in the tasks they've been given."

"Is there any way to trace this?" Roman asked quietly to the side.

"Not from here," Derek responded. "But if he's broadcasting this to everyone in Omega, then somebody's tracing it."

"I realize," Freihof continued, "that my colleagues' failures to kill the people we targeted may cause you not to take me so seriously. And again, that's my fault. Never trust someone else to do a job you really should do yourself."

Freihof, showman that he was, slowly removed the hood from his victim's head.

Grace Parker.

Roman looked into the eyes of the older woman he'd spent so much time talking to these last few months. The one who'd gotten him through not only the explosion that had almost killed him, but sorting through the feelings he had for Keira Spencer.

"Damn it, where are they?" Lillian said.

"I think that's Grace's home office. I met with her there a couple of times when I had required visits," Roman said.

Derek was already calling it in.

But Freihof was too smart to waste time now that he'd let his location be known.

"I'll make this lesson quick," Freihof said, nodding sincerely. "You call yourself the good guys, but that's not always the case, is it? It's time for you to pay for your sins."

The entire team rushed toward the screen as if they could do something when they saw Freihof take out a knife and stand behind Grace Parker.

"It's time for you to know the pain I've known."

Everyone watched helplessly as, with his words, Freihof slashed the knife across Grace's throat. She died in front of them, none of them able to do a single thing about it.

Chapter Six

An odd mixture of devastated silence and barely concealed rage permeated the air of the Omega conference room two days later. The mood inside the building reflected the weather outside.

A deadly storm was brewing.

Another one of their own was dead. This time murdered in cold blood right in front of their eyes.

Steve had called an all-hands meeting, knowing the team needed firm leadership now more than ever. Brandon Han stood at the front of the room with him. They both looked like everyone else in the room did: as if they hadn't had a moment's sleep since Grace's death and wanted to break something with their bare hands.

Preferably Damien Freihof's face.

Lillian sat next to Roman in the corner near the back. Tension fairly hummed through her small body.

"I don't know how long I'm going to be able to sit through a meeting," she whispered to Roman.

"I know. And Steve knows. Don't worry."

The room was pretty evenly divided between investigative agents and SWAT, with a few crime lab scientists and computer experts thrown in. You could tell who the SWAT team members were even if they weren't all similarly dressed in black cargo pants and formfitting dry-weave shirts.

They were the ones—like Lillian—with a furious energy flowing through their bodies. They didn't want to sit around having a meeting about how to catch Freihof, they wanted to be out there *doing* it.

But they couldn't do that, because once again, they had no idea where Freihof was located.

"Grace Parker was one of our own," Steve Drackett began. "A vital member of the Critical Response Unit and a personal friend to many of us. She'll never be replaced."

Steve waited in silence for a moment.

"Freihof has brought a war to us. To our own doorstep. We're going to damn well make sure he regrets that."

Everyone in the room nodded. A few cheered. Everyone sat up a little straighter.

"I've called you here today because I want to make sure everyone is up to speed on the case," Steve continued. "Everyone is at risk, so we all need to have as much information about Freihof as possible. Brandon."

Lips tight, Brandon hit some buttons on the keyboard of the computer he stood by and brought up a timeline on the big screen.

"Our history with Freihof goes back a long way. We thought it started five years ago when my wife, Andrea—before she was associated with Omega—was able to let Steve know about Freihof's intent to blow up himself, and a couple dozen people, in a bank in Arizona."

Steve nodded. "Grace was there that day also."

Brandon paused for a moment, nodding, before continuing. "Freihof was stopped and sent to prison, but escaped last year. Andrea and I were both nearly killed when he reappeared in Arizona after his escape." Brandon pointed to another spot on the timeline. "He showed back up here in Colorado two months ago, after not being seen for ten months."

A picture of Summer Worrall and her daughter, Chloe, came up on the screen. Roman saw Ashton Fitzgerald tense. The other man didn't like to think about what had almost happened to his fiancée, and the child he considered to be his own daughter.

"Two months ago, Freihof targeted Summer Worrall, because of her connection to us." Brandon looked over at Roman. "We almost lost Roman in the explosion Freihof set, and Tyrone Marcus died."

Roman didn't need a reminder.

"A week after that, Freihof went after our friends in Texas, Caroline Gill and Zane Wales. Fortunately, the people he convinced to target them were not able to fulfill their mission—part of what Freihof was talking about when he killed Grace.

"We had not seen or heard anything from Freihof for two months. Although we certainly had hoped he was gone for good, we knew that wouldn't be the case." Brandon looked around the room at everyone. "But things have changed now. Freihof has upped the ante."

Again, there were multiple muttered agreements.

"Freihof has decided to get his own hands dirty rather than just use other people to do his killing, the way he has in the past," Brandon said. "Up until now, part of his MO has been convincing others to do his dirty work for him. We're not exactly sure why, probably part of some sort of elaborate mind game.

"But what we do know is that he did not get the results he wanted, trying to convince others to do the killing. Their success rate was less than optimal."

"He succeeded in killing Tyrone," Roman reminded everyone.

Brandon nodded. "Yes, but Tyrone's death was not the actual plan. He wasn't the target."

"Although that doesn't make Tyrone any less dead and it doesn't mean that we're not going to make sure Freihof pays for that," Steve assured everyone.

"Freihof has now decided that he wants to do at least some of the killing himself. Grace Parker was his first target. We don't know anything except that she will not be the last," Brandon continued. "This is the note that we found at the scene of Grace's murder."

A new picture came up on the screen. A note very clearly written in bold stroked letters.

When you lose someone you love it hurts.

"What the hell does that mean?" Lillian asked. "If he thinks it hurts now, wait till I get him in my rifle sights."

There were a few soft chuckles around the room. But everyone felt the same way. Not a single person present would hesitate to take Freihof out if he or she had the chance.

Brandon leaned against the table. "We've studied the video of Grace's death. It led us to look in a different direction than we had been. Specifically, the sentences 'You call yourself the good guys, but that's not always the case, is it? It's time for you to pay for your sins.'"

A new picture came up on the screen, the photo of a beautiful blonde young woman.

"Do you think that is his next intended victim?" Roman asked.

"No." Brandon shook his head. "She was actually *our* victim."

"Our victim? What does that mean?" Lillian asked.

"It was six years ago," Brandon responded. "Some of you weren't even here at that point. There was a raid at a federal reserve in Tucson. The hostage situation had gotten out of control and we were called in."

Roman nodded. He remembered that case, but wasn't part of it. He'd been new on the SWAT team at the time, still in training.

"I remember that incident," Derek said. "The team was called in, we infiltrated the building. I think one of the bad guys was killed, and unfortunately, a couple of people were injured. And then there was some explosion, right?"

"That's correct," Steve said.

"Was Freihof one of the hostage takers in that situation?" Roman asked.

Brandon shook his head. "No. Believe it or not, Freihof was actually one of the hostages. He and his wife, Natalie Freihof." Brandon tapped the screen to draw their attention back to the picture of the woman.

Now everyone shifted a little to get a better look at her. None of them really understood what was going on.

"Okay, so psycho has a pretty wife," Lillian said. "Is she an accomplice? Or maybe we can use her to get to him?"

Brandon shook his head again. "No, she's definitely not in on this and we cannot use her to our advantage."

Roman rolled his eyes. "Why? Because she loves him so much and thinks he's such a stand-up guy?"

Steve answered this time. "No. Because she died in that bank incident six years ago."

Derek looked shocked. "What? I don't remember any report of collateral damage in that situation."

"No, it was never reported to us," Steve said. "Evidently, Natalie Freihof was caught in the explosion that took place afterward. Records are unclear. She was taken away in an ambulance and then died. No report was filed or hearing opened, because we were never notified about it."

"How the hell did that happen?" Derek asked.

Steve shrugged. "I don't know. We're trying to find out as many particulars as we can, but there are missing details about the case."

"In light of what we know, we think Freihof is blaming us for his wife's death," Brandon said.

"Did we kill her?" Roman asked.

Brandon shrugged. "We're still trying to find out as much detail about this particular case as we can. But like we said, there is information that's missing."

"So Freihof could've just decided that we killed his wife even though the hostage takers killed her, and that he is going to get revenge on all of us for something we didn't even do," Lillian pointed out.

"Absolutely." Brandon nodded. "Don't doubt that Freihof is a sociopath and doesn't need any real reason to kill people. But if he thinks we killed his wife, then he probably feels even more justified in his vengeance against us."

"And that's why he's been going after people we care about rather than just trying to pick off the team one by one," Steve offered.

It made sense in a sick sort of way. It was at least logical. He blamed Omega for taking his loved one, so he was taking theirs.

"So now everyone is up to speed. Things occurring now stemmed out of that bank situation six years ago." Steve rested his hands on the table. "We all want to catch the son of a bitch. And make no mistake, we will. But only if we work together as a team and we stay crisp."

Everybody in the room nodded and murmured agreement.

Steve turned. "Derek, you take the team and see

what you can figure out about the bank raid six years ago. Any details that weren't in the files."

Derek nodded. "Roger that. SWAT, let's head out."

The SWAT team stood, happy to have something to do that could possibly help nail Freihof.

"Roman, we need you in here for a few," Brandon said. "There's been another development I think you might want to be aware of."

Roman frowned. He didn't think he would be much help with the SWAT team, but he didn't know what development could involve him.

Derek nodded at him. "Just catch up when you're through. We're going to see what we can remember about the raid and then run the team course a couple of times to get some of this energy out."

The brutal obstacle course the team regularly ran together sounded like just what Roman needed. It was either that or punch a concrete wall.

Grace Parker's terrified face just before Freihof had killed her kept creeping back into his mind.

"How you holding up?" Andrea asked, as everyone else left the room but the four of them.

Roman just shrugged. No one could answer that question with any real honesty right now.

"I know that you and Grace had been talking a lot over the last few months," Steve said. "She was important to everyone and I'm sure important to you, too."

"Hell yes, she was important to me." Roman felt his fists clench. "And we're going to catch the son of a bitch and nail him to the wall. For what he did to her, for what he did to me. We need to stop him now, Steve."

"Believe me, that's the plan." The man rubbed the back of his neck. Roman knew Steve had to be just as frustrated at the sense of helplessness.

Brandon turned so he was half sitting, half leaning against the conference table next to Andrea. "Roman, I know we don't know each other that well, so I hope you don't mind what I'm about to say."

Roman looked over at him. "Okay."

"I didn't share all the information about what we found at the crime scene at Grace's house because I didn't think the SWAT team really wanted to know all the details about the investigation," Brandon said.

Roman folded his arms. "That's probably not a bad assumption. Not that they don't want to help or be involved, but it's just not our forte."

Brandon nodded. "That's what I figured."

"But you think I can help in some way?"

"It's about Keira Spencer," Andrea said softly.

Roman just looked at them. What did Keira have to do with Grace Parker? "Okay," he said again.

"Part of Freihof's game is that he likes to leave clues. Clues about who his next target is going to be," Brandon began.

"They found a business card from where Keira and I used to work together. It was a…gentleman's club," Andrea said, hesitantly.

Thanks to his mother, Roman already knew this. Maybe he should be grateful for that bomb she'd dropped two months ago. Otherwise it would've been dropped on him right now.

"I know Andrea doesn't announce that she used to be an exotic dancer before she came to work at Omega Sector," Steve said, "but that's actually where Grace and I first found her, and invited her to come work with us."

Roman rolled his shoulders. "Believe it or not, I was already aware of the history and the line of work." *Thanks, Mom.*

Andrea glanced over at Brandon before looking back at Roman. "I know you and Keira got a little close at the wedding."

Roman waited for the point.

"We believe that Keira might be in danger," Brandon said. "The card Freihof left had Keira's stage name on it, encircled with a heart. We think he might be targeting her next."

Roman unfolded his arms, tension tightening his muscles. "She needs to be put into protective custody. Right now."

"We are not sure that she's in real danger," Steve said. "The card, her stage name on it, the way that Freihof is switching things up. These could all be false leads."

"It doesn't matter. I won't take that chance."

Everyone's eyebrows rose at Roman's adamant tone. He didn't care. There was no way he was going to allow Keira to become the victim, even possible victim, of some madman.

He hadn't been able to get her out of his mind for nearly two months. Her beauty, her strength, the way they'd been able to talk and joke with each other.

The sex.

Everything about Keira Spencer had been damn near perfect. Roman had regretted every single day how he'd let his mother manipulate the situation. Let her use shock value to cause him to back away from Keira.

But the truth was, it wasn't just what his mother had done that caused him to do so. It'd been the overwhelming feelings he had—*still* had—for Keira that had caused him to retreat.

"Glad you feel that way," Steve said. "Because I wanted to see if you'd be willing to do some protective detail work."

Roman didn't even hesitate. "Yes."

There was no way in hell he was going to let anything happen to Keira.

And who was he kidding? He was dying to see her. To talk to her. He wouldn't have lasted much longer. He would've been searching her out, asking her to give him one more chance.

He didn't want Freihof anywhere near her, but at least having a killer possibly targeting her gave him an excuse to get near her.

"We appreciate you volunteering," Steve said. "I'm going to leave you here with Brandon and Andrea. We'll keep you updated immediately with any more information we get. And I'll let Derek know where you've been assigned."

Roman nodded as Steve left.

"I've been busy since the wedding and the honeymoon," Andrea said in her soft voice. "I haven't had a lot of time to talk to Keira in the last few weeks. She's been very busy with the salon."

Roman nodded. "Yeah, I know that place means a lot to her."

"Keira doesn't reveal a whole lot about her feelings. She's strong and resourceful, and I totally respect that about her." Andrea tilted her head sideways while she looked at Roman. "I know she was attracted to you even before the wedding, and you to her. I don't need to be a wiz at nonverbal communication to have recognized that. It fairly crackled around the two of you."

Andrea had a gift at reading people's expressions and body language. Even when they didn't want to give away information.

"Of course, your nonverbal communication right now is screaming guilt," Andrea continued, standing up from the table she'd been perched against. "So I'm wondering if we're making a mistake by sending you. Perhaps I was incorrect in the intimacy I sensed between you two."

"No, you're not making a mistake. I want to go. I will make sure nothing happens to her." There was no one else Roman would trust with the job.

Andrea nodded. "That I believe. Or at least believe that *you* believe it."

"Good. Because it's true."

"Keira might not think she needs any help. She's pretty independent," Andrea said.

Brandon chuckled. "That's putting it mildly."

Andrea ignored her husband. "But despite what she says or how she acts, she's not invincible."

"None of us are," Roman said. "Believe me, I know that better than most. I won't let her turn me away, Andrea."

"Good. Despite what anybody might think because of her past profession, Keira does not open herself up to people. I've never known her to date, never really known her to have a man around."

Roman didn't judge her for being a dancer. It wasn't illegal; she'd been an adult. If that was how she'd needed to make money, fine. He had no problem with it.

"There's something you need to know about Fresh Starts salon before you go out there," Brandon said.

"Keira started it with her own money. Bought it free and clear with the inheritance she came into when she turned twenty-five." Andrea sat back down next to her husband on the conference room table. "Keira opened the salon and bought the entire building so that no one could ever take it from her. She uses it as a sort of shelter."

Roman almost did a double take. "You mean like a battered women's shelter?"

Andrea nodded. "Yes, exactly. She provides a home and sanctuary for women who are on the run or have been trafficked."

Brandon grasped his wife's hand. "She uses the salon to teach the women a skill so they can support themselves. It's smart. Staying at Fresh Starts isn't a handout, it's a complete change in these women's lives."

Andrea smiled. "Sets their lives on an entirely new course." She stood and took a couple steps closer to Roman. "Keira doesn't talk about her past much. But she helped me live through a time of my life that I might never have survived without her. She opened Fresh Starts because it's deeply personal to her. She seems so tough, so strong. But be gentle with her, okay?"

Roman nodded, just hoping he could make up for the mistakes he'd made two months ago.

Chapter Seven

"Oh my gosh, Keira!" Annabel's high-pitched voice carried easily across the room. "You totally could've been killed."

Keira swept the body of the large spider she'd just crushed into the dustpan. "I don't think my life was in actual danger from this guy."

Annabel shuddered. "Well, you just make sure he's completely dead before coming over here."

"Don't worry, he's dead." This was one of the bad things about being the sole owner and proprietor of the Fresh Starts salon and the entire building. Anything that had to be taken care of—today it was spiders—had to be taken care of by Keira.

"You know, they say that bad things happen in threes," Annabel chirped, as she went back to the register and got it ready for the day's work. She had been one of the first women to stay with Keira at the shelter. She'd been on the run from an abusive ex-boyfriend who couldn't seem to take no for an answer. The woman was young and would be fine, Keira had no doubt. She'd become such an integral part of the salon in the last two months that neither of them were anxious for her to leave.

Even if her nonstop chatter sometimes drove Keira crazy.

The woman had short, spiky blond hair and piercings going up both ears from the bottom to the top, giving her a punk-rocker look. But her rebel appearance hid a kind heart.

"You know you should put a raw steak or something on that black eye," Annabel continued, barely taking a breath. "I know a thing or two about shiners, thank you very much, Michael."

Annabel stuck both middle fingers out in front of her toward an invisible Michael. Keira just laughed. She'd rather see a woman mad at her abuser than browbeaten by him, the way Annabel had been when she first arrived.

Keira's black eye wasn't from the spider that had made its way into the corner of the salon, but from a predator of the two-legged kind who had decided to break into the salon in the middle of the night. A vandal intent on robbing or vandalizing or something equally as nefarious.

Keira had heard the ruckus from her apartment upstairs and had rushed down to see what was going on. Blame it on sleeplessness or the terrible heartburn she'd had for the last week or just sheer stupidity, but she hadn't thought someone was actually breaking in when she had made her way downstairs. And it probably hadn't been the greatest idea to chase the intruder with a broom when she did realize someone was there. The absurdity of her plan became particularly apparent when she'd pursued the guy around the corner and he'd clocked her on the cheek as she followed him.

Thankfully, he'd left. Maybe because by that time Annabel and the other women staying in the rooms upstairs had heard the commotion and made their way down. The cops had been called and definitely eliminated any possibility of getting sleep for the rest of the night.

Which didn't help Keira's seemingly perpetual exhaustion these days. It was a lot of stress, running both a functioning salon and a shelter.

When Keira had heard Annabel shrieking from the salon this morning, she'd feared the worst. And again, still not thinking very clearly, she'd rushed downstairs into what could've been another dangerous situation.

Of course, to Annabel it had been the *most* dangerous situation. A spider. Granted, a pretty big spider, but maybe the shrieking wasn't necessary after what had happened just hours before.

"I think this is the third bad thing. If you count my phone getting stolen last week and the guy breaking in last night, and now the spider. That makes three." Keira dumped the spider into the trash can and then went back to finish her opening duties.

"But your phone was returned. So that doesn't really count as a bad thing. So I'm just afraid that there's going to be something else." Annabel crossed her fingers in front of her as if to ward off evil spirits.

"Let's not invite trouble." Keira shook her head, taking a sip of her coffee.

Then Roman Weber walked through the door.

And there was the third bad thing.

They both stood staring at each other across the room. Not unlike what they had done at the wedding.

Except things were much different now.

How dare he just waltz into her salon looking all tall, dark and hot the way he always had? As if he hadn't called her for two months.

Okay, that wasn't quite fair. He had texted her a couple times and she hadn't responded. After what had happened with his family at the country club, she'd had no interest in pursuing anything further with him.

Which was good, since he hadn't made a single move. Even though that was what she'd wanted, it had stung a little.

"Well, hello there," Annabel said to Roman. "Do you have an appointment? If not, I'm sure we can find an opening for you. You've gotten here early enough to avoid the crowd. Smart thinking."

Roman tore his gaze away from Keira to look at Annabel. "No, I'm here to talk to Keira." His eyes came back to hers. "It's important."

He said the last part as if he expected her not to talk to him at all.

Smart man.

"What happened to your eye?" he asked, as he took a couple steps closer.

"Oh my gosh. You won't believe what happened last night..." Annabel started to tell the whole story, but Keira held out an arm to stop her.

"I had a slight accident," Keira responded. "It's no big deal."

Annabel looked back and forth between her and Roman, finally realizing there was some history here that she didn't understand. Keira was just glad she didn't launch into the story again.

"Annabel, what's my schedule for this morning?" she asked.

Annabel rushed to the computer to look up the information. "Well, you have a client in about fifteen minutes, and after that you're supposed to help Heather with some techniques. It's a light day because of the storm coming."

Heather was one of the women staying in the apartments upstairs, along with her newborn daughter. A trafficking victim, she was just starting to learn some of the hair-care trade.

"Okay, I'll be in my office with Agent Weber. Please let me know when my client gets here."

If anything, Annabel's eyes just got bigger. "Oh. My. Gosh."

Keira just rolled her eyes at Annabel's words, not knowing if it was because he was in law enforcement or because he was so handsome. The other woman was nothing if not dramatic.

Keira's office wasn't very big. She didn't use it much, since both her work and her home were in the same building. It was really more of an extra supply closet that she turned into an office for situations just like this.

Situations where an insanely hot guy she hadn't seen in two months now had something "important" to tell her and might want to talk. Just what she had always envisioned this office for. She pointed to the one visitor's chair in the room and sat at the chair behind her small desk.

"I never expected to see you here again. Slumming?" Keira knew she was being unfair, but she didn't care.

Roman grimaced. "I never felt that way. Never. I don't care what my mother said."

"You couldn't seem to run away fast enough two months ago."

Roman's eyes narrowed. "That's not completely

fair and you know it. I tried to call you and text you a couple of times. I never heard a single word from you after that day at the country club."

He was right; she couldn't deny that. "Well, you didn't really try very hard, did you?"

Not that it would've mattered how hard he tried. Keira had had no intention of remaining involved with someone from a wealthy and powerful family like Roman's. That had just been reinforced when she'd done a little research after that day and discovered that his father had once been in the Colorado General Assembly. His family was the very epitome of political power.

She'd already had that relationship. Had the scars to go along with it.

Keira pinched the bridge of her nose. "You know what? I'm sorry. Forget I said that. We had a good time for a week and then it ended, and let's just leave it at that."

Roman pinned her with those ridiculous blue eyes of his. "I was an idiot two months ago. And you're right, I didn't try hard enough. But it had nothing to do with what my mom tried to insinuate."

Keira raised one eyebrow. "Oh, yeah? It didn't bother you at all when she dropped the bomb that I used to be a stripper? Didn't think that was going to taint your family name?"

Roman shook his head. "I don't care what you

used to do. Everybody everywhere has something in their past that's not their most shining moment."

"Oh, yeah? What if I consider my stripping to be my most shining moment?" She had no idea why she was egging him on. She just knew that his answers to these questions were important to her.

Although she had no idea why. Their relationship was over. Done. She'd made peace with that.

Even though she hadn't stopped thinking about him for the last two months.

He refused to get drawn into her obvious argument. She had to respect him for that. "If it was, then fine. That's what I'm trying to tell you. My mom can say all that she wants about anything you've done, or anything I've done, or anything anybody has done. But it's really none of her business."

"Well, that's all water under the bridge now. Right?" Keira didn't give him a chance to answer as she continued. "You said you were here because of something important."

He looked like he wanted to say more. More about that incredible week they'd had, that had been so much more than just a physical attraction. But she couldn't allow him to do that. Couldn't go back there and revisit those feelings. It was too dangerous.

And it wasn't why he was here. They both knew it.

"Damien Freihof struck again. He killed—brutally murdered—Grace Parker, Omega's psychiatrist, two nights ago."

Keira felt the blood leave her face. "Oh my gosh. I didn't know the woman, but Andrea talked about her. She was one of the people who first saw Andrea's potential for working at Omega Sector."

Roman nodded. "Trust me, Grace wasn't loved just by Andrea. She helped me a great deal after the explosion. Was important to a lot of people."

"I'm really sorry, Roman." Keira wished she hadn't been trying to pick a fight earlier.

He nodded at her. "That's why I'm here. At the crime scene, Freihof left a clue leading to you. A business card from your old club with your name on it. We think you might be in danger."

"Me? Why would Freihof come after me? I'm not an Omega Sector agent."

"Freihof is targeting the loved ones of Omega Sector members. Instead of coming after the agents themselves, he's trying to make us feel the pain he felt when his wife was killed."

"Was my card the only thing found at the crime scene?"

"No. The team is still working their way through other artifacts Freihof left. But Brandon recognized yours right away."

"So what does Omega Sector want me to do?"

Roman stood, as if his body couldn't take being still in the chair any longer. "The very best thing you could do would be to go into a safe house until this is over."

"I can't do that. I have responsibilities here, with the salon and other things."

Roman nodded. "I know. Andrea and Brandon filled me in about this place. About what you're doing here. That's incredible, Keira. Amazing."

Keira shrugged. She thought it was pretty awesome, too. Not because she thought highly of herself, but because she knew how important the work here was. "Thanks."

"Andrea and Brandon also told me that you'd be unwilling to leave. And I understand."

"Okay. Good. Because I really can't leave."

"I would like to give you a tracker. I know that can seem like a little bit of an invasion of privacy, but if Omega knows where you are at all times, it's a huge step toward keeping you safe."

Keira thought about that for a minute. Although she wasn't thrilled, she could see the advantages. Besides, it wasn't like she went anywhere secretive.

"Okay." She nodded. "I'm not necessarily enthused, but I can agree to it. Is that it?"

"Yes, I'll put it on your phone. I'm also going to put one on your car, if that's okay."

She handed him her cell and watched as he slipped out the battery section and put in a small transmitter.

Roman handed her back her phone, but she didn't look him in the eyes. "We also want to leave some sort of protection detail here with you 24/7. Since you and I already know each other, Omega thought I'd be a good fit."

Keira stared at him. She couldn't allow it. Couldn't allow Roman to be around her all the time.

"No."

"Keira, this is for your own safety. Freihof is not someone to be trifled with."

Right now Freihof didn't worry Keira nearly as much as having Roman as a constant presence in her life did.

"I don't mind having the protection detail here. Just not you. Tell Omega to send somebody else."

Chapter Eight

She couldn't do it. It wasn't that she didn't trust Roman to protect her, it was that she didn't trust herself around him.

What happened two months ago had thrown her for a complete loop. The feelings she had allowed herself to have for him? Those didn't come easily to her.

And then to have them jerked away again, to find out that his family was just like Jonathan's?

No, she couldn't afford to be around Roman all the time. She might end up alive at the end of it, unharmed by a psycho who was after her, but at what price? She wasn't sure her mental or emotional health could take it.

"Because of what happened between us?" Roman asked. "Look, Keira, I know I screwed up. And that's on me. But this is important. I want to make sure you are safe."

Those blue eyes staring at her with such honest intensity. With such protectiveness. This was exactly why she couldn't be around him.

A tapping on the door saved her from having to come up with the words.

"Um, Keira?" Annabel's voice came through the door. "Summer Worrall, your ten o'clock appointment, is here."

"Summer, as in Ashton's fiancée?" Roman asked.

Keira nodded. "A lot of people associated with Omega come here for hairstyles. I have to go."

"We need to finish talking about this, Keira." Roman shook his head. "I need to know you're safe. I'm the best person for that."

"I…" Keira trailed off. "I can't talk about it right now. I need some time to process everything." To find the words to make Roman understand, without explaining everything.

"Fine. I'll wait out in the car while you have your appointments today and then we can talk about it."

"No. Don't wait out in your car. You know that blizzard is coming in later this afternoon and the temperature has already dropped." He would be miserable out there. "Just stay in here or in the reception area if you want to."

He raised an eyebrow. "Is your punk rocker assistant going to chat at me the whole time if I stay out there?"

Keira couldn't help but crack a smile. "Oh, definitely. Annabel rarely stops talking, although I don't know what I'd do without her around."

"If it's okay with you, I'll just stay in here. Get a little bit of work done on my tablet." Roman grinned.

Keira nodded. She didn't want to fall back into an easy banter with him. Didn't want to remember how well they got along both in and out of bed. She felt a little dizzy at the thought.

"Are you okay?" He took a step toward her, but she quickly moved toward the door.

"Yeah. I'm fine. The last couple weeks have just been…a little crazy. And now this."

"Okay. I'll be here waiting for you," he said softly, taking a step toward her.

Keira turned and walked out, closing the door sharply behind her. Him waiting for her, with his sexy smile and sparkling blue eyes, was what she was most afraid of.

"Hi, sweetie! Oh my gosh, what happened to your eye?" Summer Worrall rushed over to give her a hug before Keira led her to the salon chair.

Keira lowered her voice to answer the question, not wanting to take a chance that Roman might burst out of the office and start searching the entire place for an unknown assailant.

"Some punk kid vandal broke in last night and I decided it would be a good idea to chase him with a broom." Keira rolled her eyes at her own absurdity.

"What were you thinking?" Summer exclaimed. "That could've been really dangerous."

Keira began running her fingers through Summer's auburn locks. "Yeah, just blame it on the fact that it was the middle of the night, I haven't been getting much sleep and I've just been acting crazy for the last couple of weeks."

Of course the truth was Keira often felt like she had to sleep with one eye open here. The women who came to stay with her at Fresh Starts often brought danger with them. The security system in the upstairs apartments was pretty advanced, but the one she'd put in at the salon was more basic. Maybe she would need to look into changing that.

"Anyway, I ran around the corner with my broom, like some Amazon warrior about to attack, and dude clocked me in the face as he was trying to get out."

"Well, I'm glad you're okay." Summer still looked worried. "I know Ashton has been thrown for a loop by what happened to Grace Parker."

"Yeah, I just heard about that. They've got to catch this Freihof guy."

"Believe me, nobody feels that way more strongly than I do."

Two months ago, Freihof had come after Summer and her toddler daughter. They'd almost been killed in the same explosion that had put Roman in the coma.

"Hey, Keira." Annabel walked over to the two of them, bringing Summer a cup of coffee. "Can I get your super hunky lawman anything while he's stuck in your office?"

Both Summer's eyebrows rose as high as they could go. "You have a super hunky lawman in your office? Anybody I know?"

Seriously, Keira was going to have to fire Annabel. Or get the girl a muzzle.

"Yeah, you can ask him," she told Annabel. "And be sure to chat with him for a while. He loves to talk to people."

There. That would keep Annabel out of her hair and give Roman a few gray ones. He could easily afford them, in all his thick brown locks.

"Um, yeah. Roman Weber is in my office. Let's get you washed so we can get you home before this storm hits."

She led Summer over to the sink, hoping that would deflect the topic of Roman. But as soon as she was back in the salon chair, Summer pressed for more details.

"Why is Roman here? I mean, it would be fine if he was here to get his hair cut. That would make sense. But I'm assuming, since he's in your office, it's not for a style."

"Evidently, a business card with my name on it was found at the crime scene involving Grace Parker."

Summer's eyes grew wide. "Are you serious? A business card from the salon? Is that who you think broke in last night?"

"No, a business card from one of my previous places of employment, not here. And no, I definitely do not think Damien Freihof broke in here last night."

Because if it had been Freihof, Keira would probably be a lot more dead than she was right now.

"But Omega Sector is concerned that Freihof might have decided to target me, or whatever." Keira got her scissors out and began to trim Summer's hair in her usual style. "And Roman volunteered to come babysit me."

She looked up from the section she was cutting to find Summer watching her face in the mirror.

"He *volunteered*? Wasn't assigned?"

Keira laughed, trying to make it seem a little lighter. "Yeah, that's what I meant. Assigned. Volunteered. Whatever."

Summer wouldn't be deterred. "So the rumors about you and Roman at Brandon and Andrea's wedding are true. That you two were hot and heavy in a corner and then nobody saw you again after that."

Keira could feel her face start to burn. "Yeah, there may be some truth to that. But it didn't last."

"Really?" Summer looked crestfallen. "I would've thought you and Roman would hit it off really well. He's a fun guy. Or at least he was. I guess almost getting blown up can change a person."

"Actually, it was more like he found out that I used to be an exotic dancer and decided I wasn't good enough for him."

Seriously? Now who needed a muzzle? Keira had no idea why she'd just said that. She met Summer's gaze in the mirror again. Her friend's eyes were huge, staring back at her.

"He said that?" she gasped. "What a jerk!"

Keira couldn't allow her to think that about Roman. Although his mother might not have been thrilled about Keira's past line of work, he hadn't ever said anything negative about it.

Keira went back to cutting hair, wishing they were talking about anything else in the world, even Damien Freihof.

"No, he didn't really say that. I can't let you think that he did. We just discovered we were from two different worlds. One of those things where it didn't work out."

Keira was absolutely aghast to find tears forming in her eyes at her own words.

Summer could hardly believe it, either. "Keira, stop." She turned in the chair. "Are you okay?"

Keira set the scissors down and rubbed a hand across her face. "I don't know what's wrong with me. I'm really not sad about Roman. That all happened two months ago. And I haven't really seen or talked to him since."

"If it's hard to be around him, you can ask Omega to send someone else instead," Summer said. "If you and Roman have a bad history for whatever reason, it's fine to ask for someone else. You don't have to be around him all the time."

Keira nodded and Summer turned back around in the chair.

"It's not that we have bad history between us. It's just that, you know…" She trailed off, knowing she wasn't making much sense.

Fortunately, Summer didn't press it. Keira finished most of her trim with the two of them talking about every other possible topic. The style Summer wanted was simple, which was good, since the other woman hoped to get home before the storm hit.

When Keira was done, she took off the cape and shook it. Summer stood and gave her a hug.

"I'm sorry I'm such an emotional wreck today," Keira said. "Honestly, it's not just today, so you can't blame Roman. He hasn't done anything to upset me."

Summer looked relieved. "Good. I didn't want to think badly of Roman, but I hate to think of him treating you poorly."

"He hasn't. I promise." Keira stretched her shoulders and her neck, then tilted her head from side to side. "It's me. I'm just tired, overwhelmed. Don't feel like myself. Have been that way for the last couple of weeks."

Summer laughed gently. "Sounds like how I felt right after Tyler died."

Tyler, Summer's husband, had been killed in a hostage situation a couple years ago.

"Of course, I was pregnant with Chloe at the time, so that just made everything worse," Summer continued. "But everything will get better, I promise. You'll find your balance again."

Keira could feel the blood leaving her face as she walked Summer to the front desk, without actually knowing what she was doing.

Pregnant with Chloe.

Keira did rapid math in her head to try to figure out when her last period had been. She listened while Summer paid for her haircut and chatted with Annabel for a minute, still trying to figure it out.

She hugged Summer again as her friend left, and promised they would get together soon.

When she'd gone, Keira turned to Annabel.

"Can you find Heather and tell her I need to

reschedule her training for a little later? I'm not feeling very well and I need to go upstairs for a few minutes."

Annabel looked concerned. "Are you okay? You look a little pale."

"Yeah, I'm fine." She walked up the back stairs that led to the apartments over the salon. She let herself into her own unit and went straight to the bathroom, reaching under the sink and pulling out a pregnancy test.

They had bought two of the tests for a woman who had come through last month. When her results had proved negative, the woman had left soon after. Keira had no doubt she was going back to her abuser. That sometimes happened.

Now Keira sat on the edge of her bathtub, staring at the unopened pregnancy test package. She never thought she would be using one for herself.

Could she really be pregnant?

She and Roman had used protection during their two days in the hotel. So it was very unlikely. It was much more likely she was just having some sort of nervous breakdown.

Keira ripped open the carton and followed the directions on the package. She set the indicator on the ledge of the sink while she washed her hands.

She let it sit there much longer than the two minutes required to give her a result.

She couldn't bring herself to look at it.

She heard a knocking on the door.

"Keira?" It was Roman's voice. "Annabel's a little worried about you. She said you're not feeling well. Are you okay?"

Was she okay? Keira could feel hysterical laughter bubbling up in her. She was still afraid to look at the results of the test, but didn't say anything.

Another minute passed before Roman knocked a little more urgently on the door.

"Keira." His voice was much more firm this time. "Open the door."

Keira couldn't avoid it any longer. She picked up the pregnancy test. A little pink plus sign shone clearly in the indicator window.

She was pregnant.

Roman's fist banged on the door again. "Keira, I'm going to break the door down if you don't open it. Or at least talk to me."

Keira couldn't stop staring at the pregnancy test.

She was *pregnant*.

The banging seemed to be blocked out by the ringing in her ears as she reached for the doorknob, to let Roman in before he broke down the door like he swore he would do.

She caught a glimpse of his very concerned face before the entire world spun around her and everything faded to black.

Chapter Nine

Roman was about five seconds from breaking down the bathroom door when the knob turned and it opened.

He wanted to lay into Keira for not answering him, for scaring him to death, when he saw her eyes roll back in her head and she started to slip to the ground.

He wasn't sure he had ever moved as quickly in his life as he did to catch her.

"Oh my gosh, is she all right?" Annabel said, peering over his shoulder as he lowered Keira gently to the floor outside the bathroom.

She seemed to be breathing fine and color was returning to her cheeks. Much better than the deathly pale she'd been when she'd open the door.

"What happened to her eye?" he asked Annabel. He hadn't pushed it when Keira had said it was an accident, but maybe this was some sort of head injury, delayed in its response.

"Someone broke in last night and she chased

after him. I think he punched her as she came around the corner."

What the hell? Why hadn't Keira told him this from the beginning, rather than saying it was an accident?

"Who broke in? What happened?" He fired off the questions at Annabel.

"Some vandal. Keira heard him in the middle of the night and chased after him."

"We need to call 911."

"No." This came from Keira, who was blinking and trying to sit up. "I'm fine. There's no need to call an ambulance."

Roman still had an arm under her shoulders. He couldn't seem to make himself move away.

"Sounds like you took a blow to the head. That should be checked out."

Keira moved from his grasp. When he saw she was going to sit up whether he wanted her to or not, he helped her.

"No, I'm fine," she repeated. "We called the police last night. It wasn't a huge deal."

"Not a huge deal? It could've been Freihof," Roman pointed out.

Her brown eyes turned to him as she sat up fully. "I think I would've gotten more than a pop in the face as I walked around the corner if it had been Freihof."

Roman couldn't argue with that logic. Not after what the man had done to Grace Parker.

"Fine, it wasn't Freihof. But you still just passed out, so maybe you need medical attention."

"Roman, I'm fine. I don't need medical attention, I promise."

He saw her move something grasped in her hand.

"What is that?"

Keira looked a little panicked. She stared at him and then turned to her assistant.

"Annabel, can Roman and I have a few minutes alone?"

The younger woman nodded, although she looked particularly pained at missing whatever was going to happen between the two of them.

"I'll be downstairs. Just holler if you need me. And I'll tell Heather about rescheduling for later."

Annabel left and Keira made her way, a little unsteadily, over to the couch. Roman looked around the small apartment.

The space was cozy, with a kitchen that opened into the living room and a separate bedroom in the corner. The walls were painted a soothing tan color and unique paintings hung on many of the walls.

Keira saw him studying the framed art pieces. "Those paintings are one of the reasons I opened this place. You know, as a shelter. They were done by a woman I knew. She was such an incredible talent."

"Was?" he asked. "As in past tense?"

Keira nodded, leaning back against the couch. "Her husband, also an artist, beat her all the time. I tried to talk her into leaving him. And she did a few times. But then he always begged her to come back. Said she was his muse. Said they made beautiful art together." Keira closed her eyes. "Unfortunately, the next time he lost his temper because something wasn't going right in his world, he had a gun. Decided it would be fittingly artistic to kill her, his beloved muse, and then himself."

Keira opened her eyes and looked at Roman again. "She must've known. Because she mailed those to me the day before she was killed. So I keep them up to remind me of why I am doing this."

"And what you're doing is amazing."

She shrugged. "The women who find the strength to get away, to change their lives. They are the ones who are amazing."

She looked so small sitting there against the couch. Keira had such a big personality, was so much larger than life, it was easy to forget how tiny she really was.

"What happened in the bathroom, Keira?" He stepped closer to the couch. "Are you hurt worse than you said? You need to tell me if that is true."

"No. I..." She trailed off.

Roman studied her more carefully. "You what? You're sick? Tired? Running the shelter and the salon is too much?"

"All of those things." She held out whatever it was that had been grasped in her hand. It looked like some sort of white pen or plastic piece. "All those things and pregnant."

Roman realized it was a pregnancy test in her hand just as she said the words. Now it was his turn for the world to spin slightly.

"Pregnant?"

"Yeah, about eight weeks, if I'm not mistaken."

"Okay, now we're definitely getting you to a hospital. You need to be checked out."

She looked over at him, a little surprised. "Aren't you going to ask me if it's yours?"

"You said eight weeks. I'm pretty sure that makes it mine."

Her brows furrowed. "Seriously, no questions to the ex-stripper about whether I've been sleeping with a bunch of different people, and how I would have to prove the baby was yours, and whether I'm trying to just get your money?"

Roman shook his head. "Whatever you're projecting right now is not my feelings at all, so just stop."

She at least had the good grace to look a little remorseful.

"And none of this changes the fact that I'm taking you to the hospital right now."

"I'm not going to the hospital, Roman. I will make an appointment with my ob-gyn and I'll get checked out. But I'm not going to the hospital."

Roman was just about to argue when there was a knock on the door to her apartment. He studied Keira as she walked over to answer it. At least she now seemed steady on her feet.

Pregnant.

Holy hell.

Roman tried to process his feelings, but it was almost impossible to wrap his head around everything: concern for Keira's health, concern about the future, trying to figure out exactly how this had happened, since they'd used protection.

Surprisingly, panic wasn't anywhere on his emotional scale.

Annabel was at the door. Another young woman was with her, and had a baby in her arms.

"Keira, I'm so sorry. I know you wanted to talk to Roman. But an emergency weather report just came on the radio. The storm they were predicting has gotten much worse."

"How much worse?" Keira asked.

"They're calling for a whiteout by later today," the woman with the baby said.

"The weatherman said people should expect to lose power and make sure they are stocked up on food." Annabel looked back and forth between Keira and Roman, worry clear in her expression.

"We have plenty of food and water. I already made certain of that," Keira assured everyone. "I just wish we had a generator in case we lose power."

Roman wanted to pack Keira up and take her over to his house. He had a generator. He had everything they required to wait out the storm.

Not to mention they had quite a bit they needed to talk about.

But he knew that Keira wouldn't leave the other women, particularly not the quiet one with the infant held so close to her. Right now, these women were looking to Keira to take care of them, and she was not going to let them down.

Whatever weakness she'd been feeling on the couch, whatever personal difficulties she might be going through, Roman could see Keira push those aside. These people needed her and she was going to step up.

Roman knew he could either get out of the way or he could help, but he wasn't going to be able to talk her out of it. So unless he wanted to move however many women were currently staying at the shelter, he needed to bring the assistance to them.

Because there was no way in hell he was leaving Keira alone. He didn't know exactly what had happened with the attempted vandalism, but the timing with Freihof was too suspicious to be glossed over. Roman would get the police report and double-check everything. But even if he found out it was some twelve-year-old, he still wasn't leaving Keira alone.

"It's too late to buy a generator now," he told them. "All the stores will be sold out. Not to mention it will be a madhouse."

Keira looked disturbed at that news, but didn't panic. "What can we do? Do you have any ideas? It was stupid of me not to purchase a generator before now."

"I've got one at my house. I'll take my truck, get it and bring it back here. As long as you don't mind me staying during the storm."

Annabel clapped her hands together, a huge smile breaking out on her face. "Yay! Now we have someone here who can kill the spiders!"

Roman looked over at Keira, one eyebrow raised. She just shrugged.

"What are you waiting for, Weber? Go make yourself useful."

Chapter Ten

Keira spent the next couple hours making phone calls to clients to reschedule appointments due to the storm. She checked the kitchen pantry and refrigerator to make sure that they did indeed have enough food.

Like many stoves in Colorado, the ones in the apartments were gas-based, so losing power wouldn't make a difference for cooking. But she had to admit that having a generator would be a big help when it came to keeping warm.

She refused to give much thought to the results of her pregnancy test. After all, there wasn't anything that could be done about that right now. There would be plenty of time to freak out later when a storm wasn't coming.

Right now, she was just trying not to panic that Roman seemed to be back in her life with a vengeance. She had no idea how he felt about the baby. She'd been so busy reeling from her own emotions that she couldn't even remember what sort of expressions had crossed his face. Panic? Happiness? Probably not. She doubted they'd have any time to talk about it over the next day or two, or however long the storm lasted. That generator was going to allow them to keep only one room warm if the power went out. Which meant everyone would be crowding around.

The "hey I'm pregnant and we haven't talked for two months and I'm not sure that we're compatible with each other but we may be tied to each other for the rest of our lives" conversation was probably not best done in front of other people.

Keira was back in her apartment when she heard a tentative knock on her door.

She knew right away it wasn't Annabel, who had a habit of knocking loudly *as* she walked in. Which had caused Keira to start locking her door if she wanted any privacy.

She crossed to the door and opened it, to find Heather and baby Rachel there. The other woman looked like she was going to start crying any second.

"Heather, what's wrong?" Keira wrapped her arm around the woman's shoulder and pulled her into the room.

"I'm sorry, Keira." She shook her head rapidly.

"For what?"

"I—I was hoping I could borrow your car."

"Right now? It's already snowing pretty hard out there."

Now Heather began to really cry. "I forgot to buy formula. I only have one can left and I'm afraid if the storm hits I'm going to run out. It was so stupid of me. I should've just gone to the store yesterday. I never plan right. I always screw up."

Keira knew there was much more going on here than just concern about not enough formula. She wanted to pull the younger woman into her arms, but knew that a move closer might throw her into a panic.

"Heather." Keira kept her voice as soft and even as she could. "None of us knew that the storm was going to grow with such intensity."

"I should've made sure I had what I needed. It was so stupid of me."

Keira reached out to touch her gently on the shoulder, but dropped her hand when Heather flinched. Keira didn't take offense at the other woman's reaction. It had been drilled into her psyche by years of abuse.

So now the woman was terrified on two levels. First, afraid that she had screwed up and that Keira was going to be mad at her, but also afraid that her infant daughter wasn't going to have enough food during the storm. The first issue would take years to address, but the second Keira could alleviate right now.

She led Heather over to the couch and handed her a tissue so that she could wipe the tears from her eyes.

"Heather, we can fix this problem. Don't worry. Okay?"

She at least looked less distraught at that. "Really? I can borrow your car? I promise I won't be gone very long."

Keira shook her head. "No, I don't want you to take the baby out in this weather. How about if I drive to the grocery store to get the formula and a couple other things we need?"

Heather looked worried again. "I hate for you to have to go out in this storm. This is *my* screwup."

"Really? *You're* responsible for all that snow coming down outside? Do you know some sort of magic snow dance I'm unaware of?"

Heather smiled just the slightest bit. Keira sat next to her on the couch, thankful when the woman didn't flinch away again.

"You're right. And yes, if you wouldn't mind, that would be great. I didn't really want to take Rachel out in the snow, either."

Keira stood up. "It's no problem, but I want to go ahead and leave now before it gets any worse."

Heather showed her the type of formula she needed, and Keira did a quick sweep of the pantry and refrigerator again to make sure there wasn't anything they were particularly low on.

They really were pretty well stocked, and Keira had snow tires on her car. So even though she was kicking herself for not having a generator, all in all they weren't in bad shape.

When she got to the grocery store, about a mile and a half away, it was a madhouse. Someone would've thought they had announced the upcoming apocalypse by the way every single food item had disappeared from the shelves. Keira made her way back to the baby section, hoping for the best, but wasn't surprised when she found that all formula, every single brand, was gone.

Damn it. She couldn't go back to the house without some formula. She grabbed some diapers that would fit Rachel, just in case, and some snack foods being sold at the register.

Keira didn't want to have to go to the supercenter, another five miles away, but didn't see any way around it.

Actually, maybe she could catch Roman in time and see if he could stop at the store on his way back. He was already out, had a lot more experience driving in this weather—because damn, that snow was really coming down—and was going to pass a lot more places on his way back to Fresh Starts.

She grabbed her phone, glad she hadn't deleted his number like she'd sworn to herself she would do five thousand times two months ago, and pressed the send button.

It went straight to Roman's voice mail. She left him a message telling him what she needed, but the message seemed to break off in the middle and she wasn't sure if it went through. She tried again, but this time the call didn't go through at all.

She texted him with the info about the formula and cursed when her phone gave the "message not sent" alert.

Looked like she was going to have to get the formula herself, since she couldn't take a chance that he hadn't gotten the message. And there was no time to dawdle.

She drove as quickly as she safely could to the supercenter. Visibility was terrible, but at least there weren't too many totally insane people like her out on the road in this weather.

The scene inside the supercenter wasn't any less hectic than the grocery store had been. Most of the food had been picked over. Unless someone was looking for cans of Spam, they were pretty much out of luck.

Keira wasn't that desperate, thank goodness.

She kept her fingers crossed as she headed back to the baby section, hoping there would be some formula. Relief coursed through her when she saw there were multiple cans left. Keira grabbed three, not wanting to take too many in case someone else was in the same dire straits.

She grabbed a couple gallons of water near the cashier's station. Just in case.

If the pipes froze at her house they wouldn't be able to get water from outside. The bathtubs were already full at home and she had a filter that could be used to make that into drinking water if needed.

But a couple extra gallons never hurt.

When Keira had paid and walked back outside, she stopped for a second, aghast. The temperature had dropped just in the fifteen minutes she'd been inside the store. The snow now was so thick it was difficult to see three or four feet in front of her.

Keira rushed to her car. She needed to get home. Now.

The car started without any problem and Keira slowly made her way out of the parking lot. But once she wasn't around any parked cars, she realized she could barely see the road at all. Seeing any buildings or getting any visual clues was completely impossible.

She grabbed her phone and entered her home address into the maps application. Without it, she didn't think she'd ever find her way to the salon. In the blinding snow, she could drive right by it and not even know where she was.

Keira fought to keep from panicking. It was like

she was wrapped in a blanket of white. Blind, but not surrounded by black.

Her phone spit out directions to her, which made her feel a little bit better. She was glad she had turned to electronic help, because evidently, she'd been going the wrong way completely.

Scary.

Keira crept along at a snail's pace, glad she was only a few miles from the salon. After about twenty minutes, she knew she should be coming up on the traffic light nearby.

Although seeing it would be almost impossible.

But when the map app started telling her to make multiple turns, Keira got very concerned. She shouldn't have to make any turns, unless there was some sort of road blockage that the map app knew about and she didn't.

She decided to trust her phone and took the left and then a second left before turning right.

She was so lost and truly starting to panic now. If her phone didn't lead her in the right direction, she was never going to find Fresh Starts in the storm.

The app told her to take another left, which she did, almost positive this couldn't be the correct direction.

When she finally saw a building, her eyes almost bugged out of her head. This wasn't the salon, it was the old abandoned church on the other side of town.

Keira drew in a desperate breath when she realized the app had taken her completely in the wrong direction.

She fought to not allow panic to swamp her. She was at least five or six miles from her house, basically in the middle of nowhere. She couldn't just stay here; she needed to get inside before this storm got any worse. There was no way she could make it back to her house, not right now, not while her phone was obviously giving her directions to some other county.

She gently turned the car around to head back toward civilization. She would stop at the first building she came to. Even if it meant she had to wait out the storm at a gas station.

She pulled onto what she hoped was the road and began to drive in the opposite direction from where her useless map app—which had never given her a problem before today; *great timing*—had taken her.

A few seconds later, a car heading in the opposite direction seemed to come out of nowhere. Keira cursed when she yanked the steering wheel to the side, then overcorrected, causing her back wheels, despite the snow tires, to spin madly on the snow and ice.

She glanced in her rearview mirror, but the car

had already disappeared in the whiteness behind her. No help would be coming from there.

She almost had the car back under control, still having gone only about ten yards from the abandoned church, when the back wheels went off the side of the sloped ledge. She hit the gas harder, to try to keep the car from slipping, but a pickup truck appeared suddenly out of the enveloping snow and smashed into the front of her car, sending it crashing down the embankment at a terrorizing rate.

There was nothing Keira could do but hang on as the vehicle careened down the hill. Her body slammed up against the driver's side door as her car hit a tree, stopping its forward motion. Upon contact, the airbags deployed loudly.

Keira sat in the unnerving silence that followed, trying to take physical stock of herself. She was alive. She was able to move all her fingers and toes. She didn't seem to be bleeding, except from where she had hit her head slightly on the driver's door window. The engine had already stalled and Keira knew there was no way she was driving out of here.

She tried to use her phone, but it wouldn't call out at all or allow her to send a text.

She had no idea what she should do. Should she stay in the car? She didn't think there was any way she could walk into town. Being out in this storm for too long would mean death. Of course, staying in this car if help didn't come would probably mean death, too.

Her only good option was that abandoned church across the road. Maybe she could at least get a fire going there. Because it was going to be a long time before anybody could find her in this weather.

She grabbed the snacks that she'd bought at the stores and one of the gallons of water. She bundled herself up as best as she could, said a prayer and headed into the white.

Chapter Eleven

When Roman arrived back at Fresh Starts, he expected Keira to rush out and try to help him carry the heavy generator. He had specifically not allowed himself to think too much about her condition—about the baby they'd made—while he was grabbing the supplies from his house.

To say they needed to have a really big talk was the understatement of the year.

But he definitely wasn't going to allow her to carry anything, no matter what she said or how strong she seemed to be.

But it wasn't Keira who rushed out into the snow. It was Annabel. And the young woman's face was full of terror and disappointment.

"I was hoping you were Keira."

Roman stopped what he was doing. "Keira's not back yet?"

"How do you know she's not here in the first place?"

"I got a voice mail and a text from her asking

me to pick up some baby formula for Heather and her daughter." Roman looked at his watch. That had been way too long ago. "Keira should've been back a while ago."

Annabel shook her head. "She's not here. I've been trying to call her for over thirty minutes. She was just supposed to go to the local grocery store."

Roman grimaced. "Her voice mail told me they were out of formula and she didn't want to go to the supercenter. That's why she called me."

Annabel bit her lip. "Then why isn't she back yet? It shouldn't have taken this long."

Roman checked his phone to make sure he hadn't missed any more messages from her. But there was nothing.

A panic began to bubble in his gut, but he tamped it down.

"Okay, I'm going to get this generator into the building, and I've got the formula Heather needs. Make sure everyone has their phones on them. Keira will call."

Roman carried the heavy generator into the salon and the women helped him get it up the stairs to Keira's apartment. Every few seconds somebody would look at their phone.

She still hadn't called.

By the time the generator was in place, Roman knew something was definitely wrong. The way Keira felt about these women, how important they

were to her, how responsible she felt for them…
she would've called.

At this point, even if her phone had died or broken, if Keira was somewhere safe she would've gotten to a phone and called someone. Or at least the salon.

"Keira's in trouble, isn't she?" Heather asked softly.

Roman didn't try to deceive her. "She would've called by now if she was somewhere that she could. She wouldn't want you guys to worry."

"She went out to the grocery store for me." The woman's face was pinched. "For formula."

Roman nodded. "I understand. But Keira is smart and resourceful. Let's give her a few more minutes and see if she contacts us."

Roman had grown up in Colorado. He was no stranger to blizzards and whiteouts. And this was a bad one. Driving back here had been difficult for him and he had a truck with chains, and fifteen years' experience driving in this sort of weather.

Even the most experienced driver with the best equipment could still be in an accident in weather like this. And it wouldn't take long for the elements to kill you if you were trapped in a car in the middle of a blizzard. Not to mention the snowdrifts could rise and cause you not to be able to open your doors.

If Keira had been in an accident, he wasn't sure

if she would stay in her car or if she would try to get out and get help.

Honestly, survival rates, based on a number of factors, wasn't good either way.

"We could try to use the phone-finding app," Heather said hesitantly. She looked like she expected Roman to scream at her for the suggestion. "Keira had all of us put it on our phones in case of…other situations."

Roman assumed "other situations" meant someone from these women's pasts coming after them. And it wasn't an impossibility. Damn it, Keira needed more law enforcement help in the shelter situation. He'd be talking to her about that, too.

Just as soon as he found her and got her out of this storm.

"Actually, that's a great idea." Roman pulled out his own phone. "But I'm going to do you one better than that. I had a tracker put on Keira's phone earlier today and one on her car."

Heather and Annabel both looked a little concerned at that.

"Don't worry," he said. "Keira agreed to it. There are some issues going on that I'm sure she'll tell you about as soon as she can. But right now, we need to use those trackers to find her."

Roman punched in the numbers to activate the tracking device on his computer. Thank God she'd agreed to the tracker before this happened. He'd never dreamed he would need it for this situation.

Once the tracker was activated, he had the application up and was able to pinpoint exactly where Keira was.

Roman's curse under his breath was pretty vile. Her car was on the outskirts of town, way past the supermarket.

"Is that where she is?" Annabel asked. "That's not where she should be, right? It's nowhere near the grocery store."

"No, that's very definitely not where she should be." Roman stood up from the table. "I need you two to call this location in to emergency services. With the storm like this there's going to be people stranded all over the place, so I expect it's going to be a madhouse for them. I'm not going to wait for them to get to her, I'm going to go there myself. But if they happen to be nearby, that's even better."

The women didn't argue and Roman wouldn't have listened even if they did. Emergency services might not get out there in time for Keira to survive. He wasn't taking that chance.

"The generator is set up and you have all you need here. When I find her, I'll contact you, so make sure you keep your phones handy. And if for any reason that dot—" he pointed to the tracker "—starts to move, you need to call me right away." He wrote down his phone number for them.

He saw them nod before he took off running down the stairs and out the door to his truck. The good news was the weather hadn't gotten any worse than when he'd arrived twenty minutes ago. The bad news was the weather was bad enough to kill a woman alone in a car, especially if she was unconscious or hurt.

And pregnant.

Roman couldn't even let himself think about that. Again. He got in the truck and forced himself to drive slowly down the road toward Keira's location, knuckles white on the steering wheel. Running himself into a ditch wasn't going to help either of them.

He squinted as he tried to see through the swirling snow. He knew exactly where he was going from the map he'd studied with the tracking device, but couldn't figure out why the hell Keira had been that far out of town. She would've had to take a completely wrong turn to end up where she was.

Of course, in a whiteout it was easy to completely lose your bearings. Keira wouldn't have been the first person it happened to.

It took him nearly an hour to drive the less than six miles to where Keira's car was located. When he got there, his worst fears were confirmed. She wasn't just stopped on the road; her car had fallen off the side and down into the ditch.

Taking a long rope, tying one end to the door of his truck and the other to his waist so that he didn't get lost in the storm, Roman walked the few yards to where the tracker had pinpointed Keira's car to be. He was almost all the way down the slope before he saw it.

His breath caught in his throat as he saw the way the car leaned up against the tree. It was a miracle the entire thing hadn't flipped when it rolled down the incline.

Roman forced the passenger door open, already a little bit difficult because of the rising snowdrift. He held his breath as he looked inside, praying he wouldn't see the worst.

Keira wasn't there.

Although relieved she wasn't hurt, he found that knowing she was out in the storm was just as terrifying. Not wasting any time, he kept hold of the rope and moved around to the driver's side of the car. Although the terrain was mostly covered with snow, he could make out where she had stood by both the front and back doors of the car, probably getting something out of the back seat. The barest of trails could be seen going around the back of the car and up toward the road.

That was much better than if she had gone toward the woods behind her, but being on the road wouldn't help much in the storm. It was perhaps possible that she had gotten a ride from someone who drove by, but if she had, she would've called.

Roman made his way back to his truck, thankful for the rope. He got inside and turned the heater on full blast, then tore off his gloves and called Annabel and Heather.

"Roman?" Annabel asked, picking up almost instantly. "Have you found her?"

That pretty much answered his question about whether Keira had called.

"No." Roman grimaced. "I found her car and it had gone down the side of a ditch, but she wasn't in it. I was hoping maybe someone had seen it go down and had picked her up."

"But she would've called, right?" Heather asked, once Annabel put them both on speaker.

"Yes, I think the first thing Keira would do is contact you if she had any way of doing that."

Roman knew he needed to put a call into Omega Sector. They would be able to access hospital reports to see if Keira or any Jane Does had been brought in.

"I'm going to make some calls and see if I can find out any information," Roman told them. "You need to stay by your phones in case she does contact you. She might not be in a situation where she has access to a phone immediately."

"We will," Annabel said, her normally jovial

tone quite subdued. "And we will let you know right away if we hear anything."

"I'll do the same."

Roman hung up with the women and called in to Steve Drackett's office at Omega Sector. As a member of SWAT, Roman wasn't usually calling hospitals about victims and wasn't exactly sure how to proceed.

If he could use his skills and sharpshooting, repelling and hostage rescue to get Keira out of this, he damn well would.

"Steve Drackett's office. This is Cynthia."

"Cynthia, this is Roman Weber. I have a situation and I'm hoping you can help me."

One of the best things about Steve's four assistants was that they were each brilliant in their own right and didn't waste time.

"Sure, Roman. What's going on?"

"I'm out in the storm searching for Keira Spencer. She's a potential target of Damien Freihof. I found her car abandoned on the side of Highway 17 on the south side of town, and I just need to know if there are any hospital reports listing her or maybe even any Jane Does that have come in in the last hour or two."

"Roger that, Roman. Hold for just a minute while I check the hospital entrance records."

The minutes waiting for Cynthia to get back to him were agonizing. If Keira was hurt badly enough that she couldn't make a phone call, then she would be in pretty bad shape.

"Roman, there's been no reports of a woman matching Keira Spencer's description coming into any of the hospitals. And no one by that name, either. With an abandoned car in the storm, I'm not sure if that's good news or bad news."

Roman scrubbed a hand across his face. He wasn't sure if it was good news or bad news himself.

"I just pulled up her tracker," Cynthia said. "Are you still at her vehicle?"

"Yes. It looks like she got something out of the back seat before she began to walk."

"Maybe she was getting some supplies?"

"That's what I was thinking."

"There's an abandoned church right across the street from where you are. Is it possible she tried to make it there? It's the only building around that she could make it to in the storm. It's what I would try to do if my options were that limited."

"That's a good idea. I'm going to make my way over there and see if there's any sign of her."

"Roger that. I'll be sure to notify you if anything comes through at any of the hospitals."

Roman disconnected the call and got his gloves back on before stepping out of the truck.

The snow had deepened even in the few minutes Roman had been on the phone. He was going to have to walk to the church because driving anywhere in his truck was impossible now. The drifts were too high.

He wouldn't be able to stretch the rope all the way from the truck to the church, so he would have to leave that behind. He grabbed his go-bag from the back, which had some food, supplies and a sleeping bag, as well as an emergency first aid kit, and headed off toward the church.

He prayed he would find Keira inside. If not, he knew he had to begin to brace himself for the worst.

That he had lost her before he ever really found her again.

Chapter Twelve

Roman made it to the abandoned church, just barely. He thought he'd been heading toward the very center of the building, but had narrowly caught the corner of it. If he'd been off by another two feet he would've walked by it entirely and probably died out there in the storm, wandering blindly.

The inside of the church wasn't much warmer than outdoors, but at least in here there wasn't the visually paralyzing whiteness.

His body shuddered from the cold. He couldn't stand to think about what it would be like for Keira, who had much less body mass than he did, and had walked farther.

And if she had been disoriented in her car, driving and relatively protected, would she have been able to find this building once outside in the elements?

The door to the church had been propped partially open, which gave him the slightest bit of hope that Keira had made it inside. But that also could've been from the wind.

"Keira! Are you here?"

It was difficult to hear anything in the vast room with the tall ceilings that seemed to magnify the echo of the winds. Plus one edge of the building had burned completely, leaving that area open to the elements, which was likely why it had been abandoned in the first place. It had been less expensive for the congregation to rebuild closer to the center of town, Roman was sure, than to rebuild this old structure.

He took a few steps farther inside. "Keira?"

She had to be here. If she wasn't there was nowhere left for her to be except out in the storm.

With his eyes now adjusted, Roman made his way forward. It looked like there were some rooms attached to the back that might offer more shelter.

As he cleared the pews toward the front of the church he saw her lying there on the ground, facedown. His heart caught in his chest as he ran to her.

"Keira." He slipped his arm under her shoulders and rolled her over so she was facing him. The pallor in her face terrified him. He ripped off one glove with his teeth and felt under her scarf for a pulse.

His breath shuddered out in relief when he found one. He brushed her hair away from her forehead.

"Keira? Can you open your eyes, sweetheart? Can you wake up?"

Keira moaned just a little bit. "Cold," she said softly.

"I know, sweetheart."

He ripped his sleeping bag out of his backpack and wrapped it around her. He needed to get her body temperature up, and quickly, but this vast room wasn't the place to try.

He picked her up, sleeping bag and all, and carried her slight weight into one of the back rooms. It was an office or small classroom or something. There wasn't much furniture left in it, but there was an old stove in the corner.

Thank God for an older church with administrators who had understood the pitfalls of a Colorado winter.

Roman didn't waste any time. He needed to get Keira warmed right away. He noticed she wasn't shivering, which was a bad sign. She was in an even deeper stage of hypothermia.

He laid her by the stove, wrapping the sleeping bag more fully around her, then grabbed the waterproof matches out of his bag and opened the stove. Some critters had decided to make a nest in there, but they were gone now. The leaves and twigs they'd left behind would be perfect to start a fire.

Roman got the fire going and went back out

into the main area of the church to bring in small pieces of wooden furniture and whatever he could find lying around. At least he didn't have to worry about the kindling being wet, or that they would run out of wood.

He made multiple trips to bring it into the room. When he had brought in enough for hours' worth of fire, he closed the door. They needed to trap the heat inside this room as much as possible. The small area would work to their advantage.

As soon as the fire was blazing as hotly as he could get it in the small stove, Roman took the sleeping bag off Keira and began unbuttoning her coat and outer layers. He needed to get her out of the icy clothes so he could get her core temperature up.

"No, cold," Keira said fitfully, as he began to peel the clothes off her. Roman made short work of his own clothes also, knowing body heat would transfer most quickly.

"I know, sweetheart. But we're going to get you warmed up, okay? Don't go to sleep. Stay with me."

He arranged her so her back was to the stove and he could lay his body, now stripped down to just his underwear, next to hers. He gritted his teeth as he put her icy fingers between his biceps and his ribs to try to give them as much warmth as possible. He did the same thing to her naked feet, putting them between his calves.

He pulled the sleeping bag around both of them, wrapped his arms around her, pulled her as close as possible and just held on.

A few minutes later, Roman gave a sigh of relief when she began shivering uncontrollably. It wasn't comfortable for either of them, but at least it meant that her body was responding and making an attempt to warm itself back up.

He knew enough about emergency medical treatment to know the shivering was an indicator that she would be fine.

Roman held onto her as violent shudders overtook her. Finally, they subsided and she was able to relax.

He estimated they'd been lying there on the floor for almost an hour when Keira finally spoke.

"I could really go for a hot bath right now."

Roman chuckled, glad to hear her say something so sassy. It went a long way toward reassuring him.

"You can have as many hot baths as you want as soon as we get home. Speaking of, I need to text Annabel and Heather and let them know you are okay."

Keira tried to sit up. "Oh my gosh, Roman, I've got to get back to the house. I've got the baby formula Heather needs."

"Don't worry, I got your message and got formula for Heather."

"That damn phone. It told me my message was undelivered. I would've never gone to the supercenter if I had known you could get the formula. And then the map app got me totally lost, which is how I ended up here on the ass end of town."

Roman chuckled as he texted both Annabel and then Omega Sector, letting them know he had found Keira and that they were relatively safe in the abandoned church.

"I wondered about that. I thought you had just gotten totally disoriented. It happens."

She shook her head. "No. I should've followed my gut. I knew that stupid phone was taking me the wrong way."

"I'm just glad you made it to this church. I almost missed it walking from my truck, which is by your car."

"Honestly, I didn't know whether to stay in the car or to come here. But since the engine wouldn't start, I figured inside a building would be better than trapped in my vehicle. Especially after that moron ran me off the road."

"He probably didn't mean it. Visibility out there is, like, two inches."

He felt her slight shrug. "Thank you for coming for me, Roman. I was in trouble."

He pulled her more fully against him. So many

things could've gone wrong, things that would have meant he wouldn't have found her in time.

Cynthia at Omega Sector texted back, asking if he needed emergency medical help.

"Let me see your fingers." He eased back slightly from Keira so that he could bring her fingers up to see them. He didn't want to call in emergency medical transportation if it wasn't needed. God knew they were required other places, for critical situations. But if Keira had any indication of frostbite, Roman wouldn't hesitate to have them sent here.

She wiggled her fingers in front of his eyes and he could see right away that frostbite wouldn't be a problem, thank goodness. When he checked her toes, he found the same.

He texted back to Cynthia that they were not in bad shape medically. She responded almost immediately. Roman broke the news to Keira.

"Looks like it's going to take twenty-four to thirty-six hours for anyone to be able to get out here to us. The storm moved in so fast there's a lot of people trapped. Emergency vehicles are trying to work the most critical cases first."

"I have some food and water," Keira said. "Although I hate not to be at Fresh Starts with the girls."

"I got the generator to them, so they should be

fine even if they lose power. And Heather has her formula."

"And I guess between the fire, junk food and water I have, we should be okay here." She snuggled in a little closer.

"I have some protein bars, too."

Once Keira knew the necessities of their own survival and those of the women back at the shelter were taken care of, she promptly fell asleep. Roman felt it as her entire weight slumped against him.

Honestly, he was amazed she'd stayed awake this long. Her body had burned more calories in the last hour trying to keep her alive than most people did in a full day.

He kept her pressed fully against him the entire time she slept. His arms wouldn't seem to let her go even if he'd wanted to.

And he didn't want to.

Maybe he dozed, maybe he didn't, but she was still in his arms when he realized she was waking up.

"Did I fall asleep in the middle of a sentence?" she asked.

Roman chuckled. "Almost, but it's understandable, given what you've been through." They both lay there in silence for a few minutes.

"Maybe that pregnancy test was wrong."

Roman froze, surprised at how disappointed he would be if that was true.

"Is that what you hope? That the pregnancy test is wrong?"

Roman realized that form of questioning was straight out of the Grace Parker playbook. Sadness hit him once again at her death.

Keira shrugged. "Honestly, I haven't even allowed myself to think about it. I mean, I love kids. I've always wanted kids, but I just didn't think it was in the cards for me."

Relief hit Roman again. He hadn't even considered that she might not want to keep a baby. Andrea and Brandon had alluded to some trauma in Keira's past, but Roman didn't know what that was.

"Why wouldn't it be in the cards for you? You're certainly still young enough to have kids."

"I guess I just always equated kids with being married, and that's not for me. Not ever again."

"You were married before?"

He felt her nod against his chest. "Yes. A long time ago. Not something I care to repeat."

"It ended badly?"

"If by ended badly you mean I had to leave the hospital with a dislocated shoulder, a broken wrist and two cracked ribs and just the money I had in my pocket, drive to another state, not use my identification in case my husband or his family came searching for me, and start my entire life over with nothing to my name?" She pulled slightly away from him. "Then, yeah. It ended badly."

Chapter Thirteen

Roman fought to control the rage coursing through him. Keira was so tiny, probably only five foot three, and couldn't weigh much more than a hundred and ten pounds. The thought of someone deliberately hurting her, breaking her bones, created a seething fury inside him.

And more so because he knew that the incident she mentioned probably hadn't been the first time she'd been abused.

"You're going to need to tell me this entire story," he said slowly. "Hopefully, starting from the end, where you tell me this guy is rotting in prison right now."

Keira gave a bitter laugh. "Unfortunately not. But he's completely out of my life and that's really all I care about."

Roman cared for a hell of a lot more than that, but he wasn't going to push it right now. "How long ago did this happen?"

"It actually started when I was seventeen. My

parents died in a car accident. The only way I can live with myself, live with what I allowed to happen to me, is by accepting that I was reeling from their death."

Roman wanted to argue that none of this could possibly be Keira's fault. It didn't matter what she had said or done. This husband of hers should never have laid his hands on her in anger. No man should ever lay his hands on a woman in anger.

But now wasn't the time to get into that. And him simply saying the words were not going to change how she viewed the situation.

"You were a child," he said. "Losing your parents had to completely shake your world. That's understandable."

"That's what I tell myself. And I know it's true."

She paused for so long Roman wasn't sure if she was going to continue, but she finally did.

"Jonathan was older than me by a couple years. He pursued me. That's really the only word for it. I was so lost and so wanting to be loved that I totally bought into it.

"After I graduated high school, I was going to go off to college. I wasn't going to stay in Colorado. I wanted to go to California or Florida or even Texas. Someplace where there was a beach." Her laugh was derisive. "Jonathan told me that we would get married and go to different beaches together. All over the world."

Roman struggled for an even tone. "That doesn't sound so bad."

"No, it sounded wonderful. I knew his family had money, and honestly, I didn't think that they were going to let Jonathan get married, at least not at the ripe old age of twenty-one, when I was fresh out of high school. But he talked me into eloping."

Keira sat up and moved away from Roman. He wanted to pull her back close to him but knew she needed space.

"I was stupid. Or Jonathan was very good at hiding what he was. Or maybe both." She shook her head slowly. "My story isn't much different than a lot of other women's. I wanted the relationship to work. I didn't have anywhere else to go.

"When he hit me the first time, we were at his parents' house," she continued, still staring at the fire. "It wasn't right in front of them, but they had to have heard it. His mom pulled me aside a little later and encouraged me not to do anything that would make Jonathan angry."

Roman sat up also, but was careful not to touch Keira. He wasn't sure if she would want to be touched now at all.

"I was mad when she said that. Shocked, because my husband of six months had just back-handed me across the face, and mad that she didn't start yelling at him."

Roman nodded. "She absolutely should've started yelling at him. More than that."

"What I didn't understand was that I was the outsider. That their family name was to be protected and sheltered no matter what." Her voice grew very soft. "What I didn't know was that they already knew their son was a sociopath with violent tendencies. What his mother said to me that night wasn't marital advice, it was her trying to help me. In some really sick way."

"What?" Roman asked.

"I don't know if her husband beat her also. Or if Jonathan had hit his mother at times. But she *knew.* She knew what he would do to me. And knew the family would protect him no matter what.

"When he beat me badly enough to put me in the hospital the first time, I thought that would be it."

Roman couldn't help it; his breath sucked in at her words. *First time. Hospital.* His rage grew.

"Jonathan's father came to see me and seemed very concerned. I was nineteen years old and didn't have any family. Over the year and a half that we'd been married, Jonathan had slowly cut me off from every friend I had." She shook her head. "So very similar to so many other women's stories.

"I left the hospital with no intention of going

home. But they had a driver pick me up and take me there, anyway. His parents were at our house and listened while Jonathan begged me for another chance."

Keira glanced over at Roman and shrugged. "Who knows, I was so stupid I might've given him another chance, anyway. But when Jonathan and his mom left the room, his dad came to me and made sure I understood that if I left Jonathan and tried to tell anybody about what had really happened, all the doctors and other medical records would show no sign of Jonathan's abuse. All they would point to were my *alcoholic tendencies*." She shook her head. "Never mind that I wasn't old enough to buy alcohol and had never had a drink in my life."

Roman closed his eyes. Took a deep breath and let it out slowly.

"Keira…" He wanted to say something, anything, to make this better. But he knew there was nothing that could be said. He got up and added more wood to the fire, needing to do something with his hands.

Besides find this Jonathan guy and give him a taste of what broken bones felt like.

"Things were better for a while after that. As always." Keira's voice became much more matter-of-fact. "Abuse tends to run in cycles. Honeymoon period. Escalation period. Violence.

"Finally, the last time Jonathan put me in the hospital, I was more prepared. I had purchased a car, a junker I bought for five hundred bucks by selling some earrings he'd given me—ironically, after another time he'd put me in the hospital. I kept it parked at a grocery store lot near our house."

Roman lay back down where he'd been before, trying to give her space. She brought her knees up to her chest and wrapped her arms around her legs. She stared out at the fire in the stove.

"When I got to the hospital, the same doctors saw me. The ones I knew Jonathan's family had paid off. But this time as soon as the doctors left, and before Jonathan's family could arrive, I walked—*staggered* is really more the word—out to the nurses' station.

"Stephanie Scott." Keira whispered the name with reverence. "That was the nurse I found. One I'd never seen before. She helped me, believed me, when I told her what had been happening."

Keira's voice grew stronger. "She helped me get documentation. Pictures of what Jonathan had done to me. Statements from several other doctors—not the ones on Jonathan's family's payroll—and everything I would need to file a police report if I wanted to.

"I don't know what would've happened if it hadn't been for Stephanie. She saved my life."

Keira straightened slightly and continued. "When Jonathan's father came to see me a couple days later to give me the normal 'we'll keep this between us' talk, I just nodded. Because I knew I had just mailed them the copies of the documents I now had, to buy my freedom.

"As soon as Jonathan's dad left, I checked myself out of the hospital and got into my little car and drove. I drove until I ran out of money and couldn't get any farther. That ended up being Buckeye, Arizona. Somebody gave me a job and paid me under the table, since I didn't want to use my regular ID."

Because her husband would've used his family's money to track her down and drag her back. She didn't say it, but Roman knew it was true.

"It bought me the time I needed to get a lawyer. Lo and behold, nobody fought me when I got my divorce from Jonathan."

Roman could only imagine how damning the evidence had to have been for her to get the divorce without a fight.

"Have you had any problems with him since?"

She finally looked over at Roman. "No. Nothing. My lawyer made sure his family understood that I would press charges if he came anywhere near me or tried to talk to me at all. I was twenty years old when all that happened. And thankfully, haven't had to deal with Jonathan or his family for six years."

"And that's why you opened Fresh Starts." It wasn't a question, after what he had just heard. "To help women who are in a similar situation as you were."

Keira shrugged. "My parents, rest their souls, left me some money when they died. But trying to be wise, they left it in a trust fund that I couldn't access until I was twenty-five."

Roman shook his head. "That money would've made a huge difference to you when all the stuff was going down with your ex-husband."

"I know." She nodded. "But in a lot of ways I'm thankful that I couldn't touch it until last year. That money allowed me to buy the salon and the building free and clear. So now all the money the salon makes can just be used to help in whatever way is needed most. No red tape. No applying for grants or stuff."

And no one could ever take it away from her. Keira had had so much taken away from her, and she had ensured that would not happen again.

And damn if that wasn't the gutsiest thing he'd ever heard in his entire life.

"I definitely could've used someplace like Fresh Starts when I first left Jonathan. Someplace where I could just get back on my feet and also learn a trade." She looked over at him and wagged her eyebrows. "Not that stripping wasn't a trade, also."

"Keira, when I let my mom throw me for a loop a couple of months ago… I'm sorry. I really don't have any problem with your former line of work. If you liked to do it, and it worked for you, then who am I to judge?"

"It did work for me. But there were some women there, Andrea included, who it didn't work for. But they didn't have any other choice. They didn't have any other options. That's what I want to do with Fresh Starts. Just give women options."

"I was coming back for you, you know," he said, his voice getting huskier.

She spun around toward him. "What?"

"This thing with Damien Freihof gave me the excuse to come talk to you. But I would've been coming, anyway. I haven't been able to get you out of my mind for the last two months."

She stared at him for a long moment before turning away. "Me, either."

"I handled it badly."

She shrugged. "We both did. Both got a little scared at how intense things became."

Roman was suddenly very aware that they were both still nearly naked in this small room.

It didn't help when Keira scooted back and lay down next to him again.

"And it was definitely intense," she whispered,

her palm finding his chest and her thigh draping over his legs.

His hand fell to her hip, his fingers clutching at the skin there, almost of their own volition.

This. This was what he hadn't been able to get out of his mind for the last two months. The feel of her skin, the curve of her waist, the brown of her eyes.

Right now, those eyes burned with the same passion he felt. Neither of them cared that there was a storm raging outside. Especially when Keira used her weight to push him onto his back and rolled on top of him, straddling his hips.

"I'm not cold anymore," she said, her voice husky. "The opposite, in fact."

"Let me help you with that then." He reached up and slid her shirt, which he'd unbuttoned earlier, completely off her shoulders and dropped it to the side.

"Twenty-four to thirty-six hours, huh?" she asked, as she trailed her fingers up his arms, over his shoulders and down his chest. "It seems to me the last time we had that much time together, we found some pretty interesting ways to keep ourselves occupied."

For the rest of his natural born life, Roman would never forget the ways they'd kept themselves occupied at the hotel after the wedding.

Hell, they'd made a baby during it. Neither of them were ever going to be able to forget it.

He reached up and gently grabbed a fistful of her gorgeous black hair, gently pulling her down to his lips.

"We've still got more to talk about. The baby. What we're going to do," he said against her mouth.

"Later," she replied. "Right now, we've got much more important things to do. Like celebrate that we're both alive."

Roman couldn't argue with that logic, so he pulled her closer for another kiss. Shifting so their hips fell together, they both gasped.

She was right. Words could wait. Their bodies definitely couldn't.

Chapter Fourteen

The floor was definitely not as comfortable as the hotel bed had been two months ago, and the food and amenities were decidedly more lacking.

But the lovemaking was equally as mind-blowing. Keira sort of wished it hadn't been. Had convinced herself that their time together had just been a fluke. That she'd imagined they'd fitted together so perfectly.

She'd been wrong. They were still perfect.

And now Keira was about to have a full-on panic attack. Maybe it was dragging up the old Jonathan mud, or maybe it was just her coming to grips with the reality that she was going to have a baby.

Not just have a baby, but have one with a man who was from a wealthy and well-connected family like Jonathan's.

Logically, she knew there were vast differences between Roman and Jonathan. The things Jonathan had done to her Roman had dedicated his life to preventing.

But that young woman deep inside Keira, the one who had lost so much at the hands of a sociopath who was called her husband, was much harder to convince.

So by the time they got the texts the next day that emergency services were on their way to the church, Keira had completely withdrawn from Roman.

She could tell he knew. Could tell he was frustrated. But she didn't know what to do to make him feel any better and still keep herself from falling apart.

He reached out to rub her arm, and before she could stop herself, she flinched. His hand fell back to his side.

"You have to know I would never hurt you," he murmured, so softly she almost couldn't hear him.

She sighed. "Of course I do. Especially after last night. But it's not always that easy. And…"

"And what?"

She could tell he was trying very hard not to let any frustration leak into his tone.

"I just don't know what we're going to do. Your family, Roman. I know you love them, but I'm not sure I can ever trust them."

"My mother may not be the easiest person to be around, but she would never have allowed a teenage girl to be victimized. Not if there had been anything she could do about it."

Keira held up her palms. "Not even to protect her own son?"

Roman seemed about to launch into a defense of his family when emergency services called out from the main section of the building, letting them know they'd arrived.

Roman's brows knitted together. "This conversation is not over. We'll table it for now, but we've got to talk this stuff through."

Keira nodded. She just didn't know what good talking would really do. At the end of the day, Roman was part of the Weber family.

They had money, they had power and they had a name to protect.

She knew Roman would never physically hurt her. But also knew that wasn't the only way she could be hurt. She'd been a victim once. She never wanted to put herself in a situation where she'd be a victim again.

Not to mention she was pretty sure that Maureen Weber Donovan would never accept Keira as a suitable anything for her son, especially not a wife. Not that Roman had said anything about getting married. Or that Keira would even consider it if he did.

The thought of marriage all but made her break out in hives.

She pushed thoughts of babies and marriage and hives aside as the emergency services team helped them get to Roman's truck and get it cleared out so he could drive. The whiteout was over, but the roads were still piled with snow.

Roman insisted on taking Keira to Omega Sector headquarters. It was closer. And they also had a doctor who could check her out immediately, rather than having to wait the hours it would take at any of the local hospitals.

An hour and a half after they arrived at Omega, Keira had enjoyed a hot shower, a full meal, and had been thoroughly checked out by the Omega physician.

None of her fingers or toes had any issues with frostbite; her pulse and breathing showed no signs of problems with hypothermia.

And a blood test confirmed she was very definitely pregnant.

The doctor assured Keira that if no damage had been done to her body from her time in the cold, then the chances of there being harm to the embryo was slight at best. Her body would protect the baby first.

She was given clothes to change into from one of Roman's teammates. Keira knew of Lillian Muir, the lone female SWAT team member, but had never really talked to her. Given that her clothes almost fit Keira, the woman couldn't be much taller than Keira's own five-three. Hard to think of someone that size on a SWAT team.

Keira's head was still reeling from the confirmation that she was definitely pregnant as she walked out, then was led by an agent she didn't know to a conference room down a different hallway.

She had no idea what she was going to do, but no matter what, in about seven months she was having a baby.

And damned if she couldn't stop smiling about that. She knew nothing was going to be easy, wasn't confident how Roman would fit into the picture, but she was absolutely positive she wanted this baby.

She'd never considered having kids of her own. She'd figured since she never planned to get married again, kids would be out of the question. Maybe down the road she would've considered adopting or something, but babies hadn't been on her radar.

They were now.

It didn't change anything for her in terms of Fresh Starts or the shelter or helping the other women. It just meant she would have another little person with her as she did it.

"Wow, that's the brightest smile I think I might've ever seen out of you." Andrea came out of the conference room and slipped an arm around

Keira. "I'm assuming the doctor said everything was fine."

Andrea was right. Keira couldn't stop smiling. "Yep. No lasting damage at all."

Her friend laughed softly. "That news seems to definitely have gotten you very excited."

Because she knew she wouldn't be able to keep it from Andrea more than a few days, she went ahead and blurted out the news. "I'm pregnant, Andrea."

Andrea had such an uncanny ability to read people that it was very difficult to get the drop on her. But Keira had just succeeded. Her eyes grew wide and she grabbed Keira's arm and pulled her down the hallway.

"You're pregnant? How did this happen?"

Keira raised an eyebrow. "You just came back from your honeymoon and you have to ask me that question?"

"You know what I mean. Who? When?" Andrea looked back down the hallway toward the conference room. "Roman Weber. I knew it."

"Do you want me to enter into this conversation or do you just want to continue to have it with yourself?"

Andrea shook her head sheepishly. "I'm sorry. Are you okay? Is this what you want?"

Keira could still feel herself smiling. "It wasn't what I was planning, but I'm definitely okay. And now that it's happened, it's definitely what I want." Her hand moved to her stomach, still completely flat, with no sign of a child inside.

"I'm going to have a baby, Andrea."

Andrea pulled her in for a hug. "And you're going to be the best mother in the world. I'm so excited for you, Keira."

Before Keira could respond, Roman was walking toward them, concern clear on his face.

"Are you all right? Did the doctor say everything is fine?"

Keira and Andrea stepped back from each other. "Yes, he said everything is fine." She looked into Roman's blue eyes. "And confirmed everything."

Andrea looked back and forth between them. "I'm going back into the conference room. I'll catch you later." She leaned over and kissed Keira on the cheek. "Congratulations, Mama."

As Andrea walked away, Roman leaned a little closer. "You told her?"

Keira shrugged. "I figured she'd be the first person I told anyway, so why wait?" All of a sudden Keira had a thought. Maybe Roman wouldn't want her telling everyone about the baby. "But maybe we should've discussed it first. Is it all right that I told her?"

"It's more than all right. Between you telling

her and that smile on your face, it alleviates a lot of my fears."

"What fears?"

He shrugged. "I don't know. That you weren't excited about being pregnant. That somewhere inside, you felt like a baby would ruin your life or something."

"No. I'll admit it's a huge change, but I'm definitely excited."

"Roman, can you and Keira come in here for a few minutes?" Steve Drackett stuck his head out of the conference room. "We found something important."

"We'll talk more about this later," Roman murmured. She felt his hand slip to the small of her back as he led her back down the hall. "But I'm glad you and the baby are fine and safe."

Inside the conference room, some of Roman's colleagues, people she'd met over the last few months through Brandon and Andrea, reintroduced themselves. Everyone was glad she and Roman were safe, but there was a somberness permeating the air that she hadn't seen before.

The reason for that gravity became apparent when she saw the whiteboard that held information about Grace Parker's death.

The pictures weren't gruesome, but they were definitely disturbing. Roman saw where Keira was looking.

"Do you want me to have them cover that?" he asked her, whispering close to her ear. "Grace's death is forefront on all of our minds so we asked Steve if we could have an open whiteboard here in case some of us, people like me who don't normally do investigative work, might be able to help."

Keira shook her head. "No, it's fine. I want to do whatever I can to help, also."

"Keira," Steve said, holding his arm out to a woman in a lab coat standing near the table. "This is Sydney Ruiz, our new computer and electronic expert."

Keira looked over at the young woman, who might be twenty years old if even that. Her youthful appearance wasn't helped by the fact that she wore her brown hair back in two French braids and was chomping on chewing gum.

"It's nice to meet you." Keira smiled.

The young woman smiled back. "Same. I've been doing some tests on your cell. Hope that's okay." She held up Keira's phone and continued her rapid explanation. "We wanted to make sure the tracker we placed would work long-term, but then I noticed some crazy stuff."

Sydney talked so fast, moving her arms around as she did so to accentuate her points, it was difficult to keep track of what she was saying.

"What sort of crazy stuff, exactly?"

"Were you using your map app when you got lost in the storm?"

That question at least Keira could understand. "Yes. I could've sworn it was taking me the wrong way, but I know with a blizzard like that sometimes you can't trust your instincts. And that app hadn't ever given me problems before."

A look passed between Sydney and Steve. This was something they had obviously talked about.

"When did you realize you were going the wrong way?" Sydney asked.

"I was pretty sure as soon as I left the supercenter, but I didn't know if maybe the app was taking into consideration some closed roads or something. After a couple of miles, when it had me do some really random turns, I seriously began to question it."

Everyone around the room was nodding and had a concerned look. Keira realized there was something she didn't know.

"Why? What's going on?"

"When did you decide to stop following the map application?" Steve asked.

"When I saw that abandoned church, I knew I was on the wrong side of town and that there wasn't much outside of that."

"Keira," Sydney said. "Have you gotten a new phone recently, or has anything unusual happened with yours?"

She nodded. "Yeah, actually, a few days ago my phone was stolen."

That look passed again between Steve and Sydney. Roman appeared concerned now, too.

"And you bought a new one?" he asked.

Keira shook her head. "No, it was turned in a day later. Somebody found it. I counted it as some sort of miracle, to be honest."

"Did you get a look at the person who returned it to you?" Steve asked quickly.

"No, I wasn't there. I'm not sure who turned it in, but they gave it to Annabel, I think. We could ask her if she remembers who did it." Keira glanced from Steve to Roman to Sydney. "What's going on?"

"Your phone has been tampered with," Steve said gently. "Whoever took it modified it to both track your location and mess with your apps."

"Like the maps app taking me the wrong way in the storm?" Keira asked.

Sydney nodded. "Exactly like that. It also would've gotten all your financial information the first time you opened your banking app. Plus, would've given the hacker information about your whereabouts when you open your calendar app."

Keira had to grab one of the chairs so she could sit in it. "I have pretty much my whole life on that phone."

Sydney paced back and forth beside the conference room table. "It was a very sophisticated program that was being run on your phone. If it hadn't caused interference on the Omega tracker, I probably wouldn't have detected the malware."

Keira looked over at Roman. "Is this Damien Freihof? Is he the one who did this?"

Roman nodded grimly. "Almost positively."

"Did anything else happen to you while you were out in the storm?" Steve asked. "Before Roman got to you?"

"I got run off the road. I don't know if that counts. But it might've just been from people like me who couldn't see anything. Although..."

Now that they were talking about bad guys and someone hunting her, she wasn't sure if she was just letting her imagination get the better of her.

"What?" Steve asked. "You tell us everything and let us sort out what may be deliberate and what may just be part of a weather-related event."

Keira told him about the car that had almost hit her as she pulled away from the church and then the pickup that she felt had been deliberately trying to hit her.

She shrugged. "Thinking someone was deliberately trying to run me off the road seemed ridiculous and extreme at the time. But now..."

But now there seemed to be a madman intent on destroying Keira's life, the way he had so many others.

Chapter Fifteen

The next two weeks passed in a blur for Keira. Brandon came back to Fresh Starts with her and Roman to interview Annabel about the person who had turned in Keira's phone after it had been stolen.

Unfortunately, all Annabel remembered was that it had been a sort of old man, nondescript, who didn't say very much.

"He just told me he found it outside near a trash can. I was so excited about it being returned that I didn't think to question him about it. He didn't look like a criminal." Annabel wrung her hands as she answered the questions.

Keira slipped her arm around the other woman's shoulder. "Why would you have any reason to suspect him? You thought it was a Good Samaritan turning in a lost item."

But after talking to Roman and Brandon, Keira realized that the old man could very definitely have been Damien Freihof. They'd shown her some pictures of what he'd looked like at different places. Evidently, the guy was a genius with disguises.

Omega Sector also sent some of their forensic team to check for prints from the vandal who had broken in the night before Keira found out she was pregnant. They did find some prints, but they weren't in the system.

That was both good and bad news. Good, because Freihof's prints were in the system and they weren't his. Bad, because that was another dead end.

And since Freihof often used other people to do his dirty work, the person who broke in may not have been a vandal or burglar at all. Once again, Keira was very thankful she'd gotten only a black eye. Could've been much worse.

They installed a much more sophisticated security system in the salon. It had been costly, but worth it.

Between getting all this done, running the salon and dealing with the issues the women staying in the shelter had, and oh yeah, being pregnant, Keira was exhausted.

The only thing she knew for certain was that Roman was there every time she turned around.

Literally.

When they left Omega Sector after the storm, Roman had wanted Keira to come home with him.

"We can't underestimate Freihof," he'd said. "I want to protect you and the baby. I can do that best at my house."

She'd been tempted, she really had. But she couldn't.

"There's nothing I'd like better than to hide out until this entire thing blows over. But I can't. These women need me and I couldn't live with myself if I was just another person who let them down."

Roman didn't get angry, he didn't push. She appreciated that.

But he did go back to his house so that he could pack a bag to stay with her at the salon.

"I can't make you stay with me. Honestly, I don't even want to try to make you stay with me. You're right, those women are counting on you." He turned his blue eyes on her. "But until Damien Freihof is caught, I will be staying here, too. Not some other random agent. Me. Deal with it."

It was a confusing thing to be irritated and so completely turned on at the same time. But Roman did that to her when he got all alpha male.

Plus having him here had meant a measure of relief that Keira could hardly allow herself to admit. A sharing of the burden.

Yesterday, when Annabel had found another spider and screamed bloody murder, calling for Keira, Roman had rushed into the salon, weapon drawn. When he'd seen what the actual danger was, he'd just rolled his eyes.

Then killed the spider.

Keira had to admit it was nice. She'd been doing everything for herself for so many years, what felt like forever, she hadn't really known how nice it could be.

She and Roman hadn't made love since they'd been trapped during the storm. Keira just needed space and Roman had again respected that. Hadn't pushed.

Which, of course, just made her want him more. Everything about him seemed to make her want him more. The way he treated the women staying at Fresh Starts with gentleness and respect. The way he was able to see what needed to be done and just did it. That sometimes involved installing further security measures and sometimes involved picking up a broom and sweeping the floor.

Roman never had to be asked to do it, he just did so.

And when Keira saw him holding Heather's baby, with such obvious gentleness and joy, something inside her cracked wide open.

Concerned about her, he'd asked Keira if having the baby would change her life. But she hadn't asked him if he was concerned about a child changing his own life. Now, seeing him hold baby

Rachel was just evidence of what a good father he was going to be.

Two weeks after the storm, they were eating takeout in Keira's apartment after a late night salon closing. Roman was telling a hilarious story about how he'd locked his sister in the bathroom after she quit a Monopoly game in the middle of it once it became apparent she was going to lose. Keira was laughing so hard her sides hurt when they heard it: the breaking of a window in the salon and the alarm blaring.

Within seconds everyone was running down the stairs.

Roman stopped them. "Everybody back. Keira, take everyone into your apartment and lock the door."

Keira's eyes flew to his. "Do you think it's Freihof?"

"I don't know. But I can do my job much more effectively if I know you all are safe."

Keira nodded, even though she didn't like it. He was right. The best thing she could do to help him now was to get everyone out of his way.

She turned to the women. "Let's go, ladies. Back into my apartment until we know what's going on."

Rachel was crying as Keira led Heather, Annabel and the other two women who had recently joined them at the shelter into her apartment.

A few minutes later the alarm shut off. It wasn't long before Roman came and knocked at the apartment door.

"It's okay for you all to come out," he said. "It looks like a rock got thrown through the window. That's what set off the alarm."

Keira hadn't given the other women all the details about Damien Freihof, but they knew there was someone out there who wanted to harm her.

Of course, all these women had someone out there who wanted to harm them. So none of them had been surprised to find Keira did also. Brenda, who had just moved to the shelter two days ago, glared at all of them.

"I'm leaving. This place isn't any safer than the homeless shelter downtown. Maybe even more dangerous."

Keira felt heartbroken, but didn't try to argue with the woman. She needed to go where she felt safe. Maybe all the women needed to go somewhere else until this was over. Maybe Keira needed to close the salon.

But no one else made any similar statements. The other women gave Keira a hug and headed back to their rooms. Annabel smiled and told her not to worry, it was only a rock. But Keira could see the tension in her face.

She turned to Roman when they were alone.

He pulled her into his arms. At first she resisted, but then allowed herself to sink into his strength.

"How bad is it?" she asked after a long minute.

"Damage-wise, not so bad. The rock was thrown through the side panel window, not the main one. So you should be able to get it easily replaced tomorrow."

Keira let out a sigh. "I need to go down there and check it out."

Roman didn't let her. "The forensic team is coming by to search for any trace evidence. Don't go down there yet."

"Could it have been an accident? I don't know a lot about Damien Freihof, but I don't think his style seems to be throwing rocks through windows. Maybe it was that vandal I stopped last week."

"It definitely wasn't an accident or a vandal."

"How do you know?" She pulled out of his arms. "There's something you're not telling me, isn't there?"

Roman nodded. "The rock had a message written on it."

"What?" she asked. "What did it say?"

Roman grimaced. "'I'm coming for you, bitch.'"

"Oh my gosh, Roman. Do you think it was Freihof?"

Roman's face was tense. "Rocks through a window aren't his normal MO, but it definitely could be. Or it could've been—"

The screaming coming from down the hall startled them both.

"That's Heather," Keira whispered, aghast.

"Stay here."

"There's no way in hell, Weber."

Roman took off running down the hall, but Keira was right behind him. When they got to Heather's room, the door was cracked open.

Peeking from behind Roman, Keira could see that a strange man was holding Heather in front of him with a gun at her head.

Roman had his weapon raised and pointed at the man instantly. "You need to drop that gun right now."

The intruder's eyes grew wilder. "No way, man. Do you know what this bitch has cost me? She was one of my best tricks."

Keira looked at Heather again. The woman was crying, her face totally white, but at least she didn't have the baby in her arms. Little Rachel must be over in her crib.

"Keira—" Heather called out, raising her arm toward the crib, before the man jerked her closer.

"You shut up, bitch. You've caused enough trouble. I didn't think I would ever find you, but you didn't run far enough, did you?"

This man was obviously dangerous. But Keira

knew what Heather wanted her to do, and she was going to do it.

She started to move from behind Roman into the room.

"Keira, stop." Roman's voice was tense and so low only she could hear it.

"I'm getting what matters most to Heather out of the room. Then I'll leave you to do your job."

Keira kept her hands raised as she eased along the wall toward the crib.

"What the hell are you doing?" the man asked wildly.

"I hired Heather as the nanny for my baby." Keira knew she couldn't let this maniac know that Heather had a child in the room. "So I want to get my baby out of here because I don't like guns."

Keira didn't look at him again as she marched over to the crib and picked up baby Rachel. She prayed the man would buy her story and she could get the child out of the room.

"Mama's here," Keira said in a singsong voice as she lifted the baby from the crib. "Let's get you out of here."

As Keira crossed back to the door, she got a glimpse of the man's face. He obviously had believed her and was just looking at her with distaste.

Heather's face was so full of relief it brought tears to Keira's eyes. The woman didn't care what happened to herself, only what happened to her daughter. She was desperate that this man not know about the child.

Once Keira and Rachel were behind him, Roman took a step forward. "Drop the gun. Right now," he said.

Keira forced herself to keep quiet as the man tightened his choke hold around Heather's neck with his arm.

"I traveled over fifty miles to find this bitch. I'm taking her back with me. This ain't got nothing to do with you, mister. Your baby is safe, so why don't you just let me leave with my...employee."

More tears streamed out of Heather's eyes. She obviously thought Roman was just going to let the man take her.

"Can't do that. I'm a federal officer. You picked the wrong house to break into."

The man considered how this changed the gravity of the situation. It didn't take a genius to figure out he was going to kill Heather.

But Heather realized it, too. And, based on what Keira knew about her past, about how ashamed she felt that she had never physically fought back against the man who had taken her and forced her to become a prostitute, Heather did something she'd been wanting to do for a long time.

She swung her arm out and with all her might elbowed her captor in the gut.

He obviously wasn't expecting that. When he doubled over and Heather stumbled to the side, Roman took a shot. He fired into the man's shoulder, which caused him at once to drop the gun.

Heather scrambled away as Roman leaped for the man, dragging him down and away from the woman and the weapon.

The man began screaming as Roman pinned his arms behind him, keeping his head forced to the ground with his knee.

"Heather, go get my handcuffs in Keira's apartment. I can promise you you're never going to have to worry about this guy ever again."

Chapter Sixteen

That night Roman slept in Keira's bed.

He hadn't minded sleeping on the couch all the nights before. In fact, in a lot of ways he thought it was healthy. He and Keira needed to establish a normal baseline.

Moreover, she needed to learn that she could trust him. That he wasn't going to rush her or force her into anything she wasn't ready for. The greatest way to do that was to give it time.

As part of the SWAT team, a lot of times he had to make split-second decisions that meant life or death. But more often than not he had to wait, use an uncanny patience, in order to achieve the results the team needed.

He didn't necessarily enjoy it, but he knew how to be patient. And Keira was worth being patient for.

Wrapping up the attack at Fresh Starts took hours. It was long after midnight by the time they finished the police and paramedic business, and Roman had filed his report for discharging his weapon.

Roman hadn't resisted one bit when Keira had pulled him into the bed with her. He just held her as they both fell into an exhausted sleep.

He was still holding her against him when a call from headquarters pulled him out of his sleep. Evidently, Heather's attacker was out of surgery, awake, and wanted to see if he could cut some sort of deal.

Brandon Han would be questioning him and needed Roman there, too. Roman didn't ask why, just got ready.

Keira's small body clung to him as he left the bed. He whispered to her that he had to leave, but when she made no real move to wake up he just smiled and left her sleeping. He wrote a note and left it on the pillow beside her so she would know where he was when she awoke.

When Roman arrived at the hospital, Brandon handed him the guy's rap sheet. "Ronald Dunham, aka Spike."

Roman glanced through the file. It was a virtual laundry list of crimes. Battery, willful destruction of property, assault. He was also wanted for suspicion of human trafficking in three different states.

"This guy's a real prince," Roman muttered. "I have no doubt he would've killed Heather if I hadn't taken him out."

Brandon nodded. "Me, either. He's done some stints for lesser crimes. But I think he realizes now he's about to face some real charges. This is Sean Smallman with the DEA." Brandon gestured to a man walking up with a cup of coffee. "Sean and I have a plan."

Sean shook Roman's hand as Roman raised an eyebrow. "I hope this works, Han. There's no way we're letting Dunham walk out of here free."

"It'll work. And trust me, we don't want Spike free, either."

Roman looked back and forth between the two men. "What's the plan?"

"Spike mostly works out of Salt Lake City and Vegas," Sean said. "Although we are pretty sure he has a trafficking ring in Denver also. We have the evidence, just have never been able to catch him."

"Okay. Are we going to make a deal to get info about other traffickers? Try to turn this guy into an informant? I'm not sure that will work." Roman thought of the gun pressed to Heather's head. "And I'm not sure it's worth it."

"Don't worry." Brandon's smile held nothing close to amusement. "Spike is making a deal with Omega Sector for us to drop charges for what happened at Fresh Starts. That you specifically won't be pressing charges for him breaking in with a weapon. I'll need you here to reassure him of that."

"I'm willing to do that." Roman nodded. "But not if it allows him back out on the streets."

"It won't." Sean grinned so hard it had to hurt his teeth. "As soon as you're finished with your deal, I'll be arresting him on trafficking charges. We have enough to put him away for almost the rest of his life."

"Good. Because if Spike gets out of here, he'll be back at Fresh Starts the first chance he gets."

Branded nodded. "That's what got me thinking about this possibility in the first place. Fresh Starts is not a known shelter. It's not big enough or established enough to be a place someone like Spike would know about."

"So how did he find out about it?" Roman asked. "Because he knew just what to do to get inside."

"It seems like someone called Spike and offered him the information."

Roman grimaced. *"Freihof."*

"My thoughts exactly."

It fit perfectly with Freihof's MO. Bringing someone else in to do his dirty work.

"All right." Knowing Freihof was involved upped Roman's sense of urgency. "Let's see what our friend Spike has to say."

Brandon and Roman walked into the hospital

room, where Spike's good arm was handcuffed to the bed. The DEA agent stayed out of sight. Important if this plan was going to work.

"That's the guy!" Spike yelled. "That's the guy who used unnecessary force and shot me."

Brandon very calmly closed the door behind him and walked closer. "We both know that's not going to work, Spike. There are two other witnesses that said you had a gun to a woman's head."

Spike immediately dropped the victim act. "Bitches. You can't trust anything they say," he muttered. But he didn't continue to argue about unnecessary force.

"Agent Weber is here to sign an agreement that he won't press charges against you for pulling a weapon on a federal officer," Brandon told the man. "There will be no charge of assault with a deadly weapon. But in return, we want more information about how you found the woman you were looking for."

Spike's eyebrows shot up. He hadn't been expecting this. The man had obviously thought he was going to have to roll over on some of his friends and colleagues in the trafficking trade.

That might still happen, but it would happen with the DEA, not with Omega.

Giving up information about someone like Freihof, to whom he had no real ties? That obviously wasn't going to be a problem for Spike.

"Okay, sure. You sign the papers and I'll tell you what you want to know."

"Spike," Brandon said. "I know you were read your rights when you were first arrested. But you should know you have the right to have an attorney with you now."

This was the moment of truth. If Spike was smart enough to call a lawyer, this plan wouldn't work.

"All you want is info about the guy who called me?" Spike asked, the hair his nickname came from sticking straight up in clumps against the hospital pillow.

"That's it." Brandon nodded. "Omega Sector's sole interest and questioning of you will have to do with the man who called you. Only him."

A lawyer would've pointed out to Spike the gaps in the agreement. That Brandon had made the agreement just for Omega Sector, not for all law enforcement agencies.

But Spike was too cocky to bring anyone else in. Thought he had it all under control. He relaxed against the pillow.

"Yeah, sure. You've got a deal."

Brandon got out the paperwork he'd already drawn up and explained it to Spike. As a measure of "goodwill," Brandon even took off the handcuffs.

The younger man looked like the cat who ate

the canary. He obviously thought he was going to get away with the scam of the century. Couldn't wait to get back and tell his buddies about his close call.

Roman just wanted to know about Damien Freihof. But he knew he had to let Brandon do his job.

Brandon was almost always mentally two steps ahead of everyone else in the room. He was a dozen steps ahead of Spike.

"So tell us about the phone call you got which led you to Heather's location," Brandon began.

Spike shifted his eyes over to Roman and smiled, since he thought there was nothing Roman could do to him now. "I was in Denver a couple of days ago and I got a text. Someone said they knew where Heather was."

Spike looked back at Brandon. "Heather and I had a falling-out seven or eight months ago. I just wanted a chance to tell her how sorry I was that things went so bad."

Roman barely refrained from rolling his eyes. He remained where he was, near the door.

"I texted the person back and said I wanted to know where Heather was. Guy said he couldn't tell me over the phone, but wanted to meet."

"So you just met a complete stranger who was doing you a good deed?" Brandon asked. "No offense, but you seem too smart to fall for something like that."

Spike smiled, not realizing Brandon was playing him like a fiddle.

"That's right. I am too smart. I met with the guy, but made sure I had lots of…friends with me. Just to make sure this wasn't some sort of trick."

"And the guy gave you the information? Didn't want anything from you in return?" Brandon asked.

"He just said he wanted to make sure some damage was done to the haircut place. A rock through the window. Made me promise not to hurt anybody else, just wanted to shake things up."

"And this man you talked to? What did he look like?"

"I don't know, man. I guess he was about six feet tall. In his thirties or forties. Brown hair. I think he was pretty strong, but he didn't want to show it off, you know?"

Brandon pulled out a picture of Damien Freihof from the file. "Is this the man you spoke with?"

Spike took the picture and studied it for a minute. "Yeah, I think so. I mean, he didn't look exactly like this, but the eyes… The guy I talked to had the same sort of eyes. Kind of dead, you know? Like he didn't have anything left to be afraid of."

Roman wasn't surprised to hear that it was Freihof who had given Spike the information. But that didn't actually help them catch him. All it did was provide them with information they already had: that Freihof was targeting Keira.

"Is there anything else you can tell us about this guy?" Brandon asked. "Anything you remember about him? More information you might've received from him?"

Spike looked back and forth between Brandon and Roman for a long time, obviously trying to consider how much information he should share. "Why you want this dude?" he finally asked.

Brandon took a step toward Spike. "This guy has killed seven different people that we know of. Including one man who was his partner. He also tried to blow up a bank full of people a few years ago. Arresting him is of primary importance to us."

Roman could appreciate what Brandon was doing. He was making Spike think Omega Sector had much bigger fish to fry than him. Which was nothing but the truth.

Plus, they would just let the DEA fry Spike.

"All right, look, I've got this kid who works for me. He's, like, twenty years old, but he looks like he's twelve. Small kid. Rico. He's awesome at following people."

Spike ran his good hand through his hair and continued. "Like you said, I'm too smart to just get drawn in by someone giving me something for nothing. I met with this guy, he gave me the information and said he didn't want anything. But I had Rico follow him."

Roman pushed away from the door. Now they were actually getting some possibly useful information.

"Rico followed this man in Denver? Knows where he went?"

"More than that, man." Spike's eyes darted to Roman. "Rico followed him all the way back here to Colorado Springs. All the way to his town house. I wanted to make sure the guy wasn't a cop or wasn't working for one of my competitors."

Brandon looked over at Roman, then back to Spike. "You know where this man lives? Here in town?"

"Yep." Spike rattled off an address on the south side of Colorado Springs. A group of town houses. "I know he was there as of last night. Rico reported in before I had my lapse in judgment and went to talk to Heather."

Brandon stopped questioning the man and turned to call in the information to HQ.

"Hey, does this mean I'm free to go?" Spike asked.

"Yep," Brandon said. "Omega Sector has no further holds on you."

Roman turned to leave, so he could make it back to Omega Sector to be part of the SWAT team that closed in on Freihof's town house.

As he was running out the door, he could hear the DEA agent coming and arresting Spike on the other, much worse charges. Spike wasn't going anywhere but to prison for a long time. He was already yelling about being tricked and the un-fairness of it all.

But Roman didn't give a damn about Spike. He wanted Freihof.

And this time they had him.

Chapter Seventeen

Eighty-eight minutes later, Roman sat in a nondescript van parked half a block from Damien Freihof's town house. Three members of the SWAT team waited with him: Derek Waterman, the team leader, Lillian Muir and Liam Goetz. All of them were as focused as Roman.

Ashton Fitzgerald, the team's sharpshooter, sat somewhere on a roof above and across the street from the town house, ready to take a shot if Freihof was positively ID'd and tried to run. Freihof was not going to be given a chance to kill more people by getting away today. Deadly force had been authorized.

Other Omega agents were in the back alley behind the town house and finishing the process of clearing people out of the units surrounding Freihof's.

SWAT would be infiltrating in less than two minutes.

This situation was why the SWAT team worked

together day in and day out with training exercises. Every single person knew what they were supposed to do in these conditions. Knew each other's strengths and weaknesses. Knew how to have each other's back in a firefight without any words needing to be said.

This is what they did.

Everyone, including Lilian, who was barely more than a hundred pounds herself, wore the forty pounds of gear standard for a SWAT team. They all had an assault rifle as well as sidearm, ballistic vest, helmet and various tactical aids that hopefully wouldn't be needed.

With the size of the town house, it had to be a small team working their way inside. Roman and Lillian would be coming in the back door, Derek and Liam taking the front.

"In order to not give Freihof any heads-up, we're using ballistic breaching to get through the doors. Move in quickly and watch your six," Derek said.

That was fine with Roman. Ballistic breaching meant shooting out the locks on the door. It wasn't the safest method of breaching, but it was damn well the quickest.

"All right, let's move out," Derek said, once he'd been given the signal that the area had been cleared of civilians. "I know we all want to nail him in the worst possible way, but everybody stay frosty. Freihof is not our normal run-of-the-mill bad guy."

The team nodded and moved out of the van, working their way the short distance down the empty block to the row of town houses. Roman and Lillian silently moved around to the back as the others went to the front.

"All's quiet from up here," Ashton said into the communication earpiece from his perch up on the roof.

"Everybody ready?" Derek asked.

"Roger that," Roman said. The other team members echoed his sentiment.

"On my mark," Derek muttered.

Roman and Lillian nodded at each other. Lillian would shoot out the lock and Roman would kick the door in.

"In five, four, three, two, go go go!"

On Derek's mark, Lillian shot near the door's lock and a moment later Roman kicked it in.

Roman's automatic rifle was up to his face as he turned to one side, and Lillian followed behind him, turning the other way.

"Clear," Roman said quietly, after he had looked around the kitchen to make sure no one was in there.

"Clear," Lillian echoed.

Roman tapped her on her shoulder and pointed to the closed door of the pantry. Lillian nodded and they made their way toward it. Roman got into position to open the door and Lillian counted down with her fingers.

Three, two, one.

Roman snatched open the door and Lillian moved in low. The room was also clear. They silently moved to the living room. No one was there, either.

Through their communication devices, they could hear Derek and Liam moving into the bedrooms upstairs. Like the downstairs, no one was there.

"We are completely clear down here, Derek," Roman said, when he heard Derek and Liam finish their search.

"Yeah, he's not here, either, but this is definitely Freihof's place. He's basically got a war room against Omega up here."

"Do you think he just got lucky? He just happened not to be home?" Lillian asked, still looking around, as they all were.

Roman moved back into the kitchen. A half-cooked egg sat in a pan on the stove. Roman took off his glove and held his hand over the pan. The oil was cool.

Freihof had left in a hurry, but it hadn't been in the last few minutes. It hadn't been because he'd realized law enforcement was clearing the block.

Damn it, Freihof had been tipped off.

"Derek, we've got a problem here. Somebody let Freihof know we were coming. He was in the middle of cooking—"

"Everybody out. Right damn now!" Liam's yell pierced their eardrums. "We just tripped some sort of explosive device and it's going to blow."

Roman and Lillian were running for the back door as they heard Liam's surprised curse as he stumbled down the stairs.

"What the hell?"

"Liam's down," Derek muttered. "There was some sort of nerve agent around the explosives that got him when he backed away."

Without a word, Roman and Lillian rushed back through the kitchen to the stairs. There was no way they were leaving anybody behind, even if it cost them all their lives. They distributed Liam's weight among the three of them and ran back down the stairs.

Unconscious as he was, Liam's weight wasn't insignificant and they were barely out the front door when the entire building blew. The heat and pain seared through Roman's mind, so similar to what had happened to him two months ago.

The force of the blast threw them all forward, Liam flying farthest of all. The world spun.

"Status! C'mon, you guys, someone report."

Roman's senses returned as Fitzgerald's panicked demands rang in his ears.

"Fitzy." Roman barely got the word out. He felt like someone was sitting on his chest, making it difficult to draw in air.

"Roman?" Fitzgerald's voice was frantic, his breathing ragged. "I'm on my way down."

Roman struggled to get his bearings through the ringing in his ears and the smoke everywhere. He could see Derek sitting up a few feet away with the same dazed look. They gave each other a slight nod, signaling that they didn't think they were seriously injured.

"Fitzy, ambulance for Liam." Roman's voice sounded odd to his own ears.

"It's already on its way. Good thing we cleared out those other town houses because the explosion took the units on either side."

Roman hadn't wanted to wait. He'd wanted to move in on Freihof before they cleared the other buildings. But Derek had gone by the book, and thank God. Maybe they would've caught Freihof if they'd been here ten minutes sooner, but it would've cost innocent lives and wouldn't have been worth it.

Derek dragged himself over to Liam, who was still unconscious. Roman heard a stream of vile curses come from Lillian, just behind him. He crawled over to her through the smoke to find her lying on her side, still muttering every curse word he knew and a few he didn't.

"Lil, you okay?"

"I'm alive and not brain damaged, so I guess that counts for something," she said through gritted teeth.

As Roman got close enough to her to see the problem, he blew his breath out in a whistle through his teeth. A shard of glass protruded from Lillian's shoulder. The part he could see was at least eight inches in length and an inch or more in width. Roman didn't touch it, knowing that he couldn't remove the shard of glass without doing more damage than good.

"Hey, you've got a splinter in your shoulder," he said, easing himself closer.

Lillian gave a low laugh. "Yeah, just one more scar to add to my collection. Guess I won't be wearing any strapless dresses for a while."

Roman lay down beside her, feeling better now that a full course of oxygen was getting through his system. Unlike the last explosion Freihof had left for him, it looked like Roman was going to be able to walk away from this one.

But not Liam and Lillian.

Roman could hear sirens in the distance. They would be here soon.

"Liam?" Lillian asked through gritted teeth.

"Alive. Breathing but not conscious." Derek's voice came through their comm units.

Ashton made it down to them and directed the

ambulances as they arrived. Roman just sat with Lillian. She had to be in tremendous pain, but aside from the occasional curse she didn't complain at all. But by the time they got her onto the stretcher her face was devoid of color. Even her lips were white. She didn't say anything to Roman as they wheeled her away, still lying on her side, just gave him a small nod.

Liam had been loaded onto the very first ambulance to arrive and taken immediately to the nearest hospital. Until they knew what sort of nerve agent or reactant Freihof had placed on the explosive, Liam would be considered in critical condition.

Both Roman and Derek were briefly checked out, but they'd had enough injuries over the years to know when they weren't seriously hurt. They both stood looking at the wreckage of what used to be Freihof's home.

"He knew we were coming, Derek," Roman said, shaking his head. "He didn't just get lucky and happen not to be here. He left stuff on the stove top."

"Someone tipped him off."

"Exactly. And given the short amount of time between when we got the information from Spike and when we arrived on scene here? That means the mole inside Omega is an actual person."

Derek scrubbed a hand over his face. "Not

some sort of computer leak or something like that. Somebody we know and work with every day is a traitor."

"And we're not going to be able to stop Freihof until we figure out who that is."

Derek muttered a curse under his breath. "Now it looks like we have two deadly bad guys to deal with. Let's get back to HQ and debrief, and let Steve know what we are thinking. Then we need to get over to the hospital with Liam and see what's going on. I've got to call Vanessa."

Roman nodded. Calling Liam's wife, and mother to their three children, wasn't going to be easy. Hopefully, it wouldn't be to the worst news possible.

Freihof, and whoever it was he was working with, had just scored another big hit against Omega Sector.

Chapter Eighteen

The day was chaotic at Fresh Starts.

After the late night with Spike's attack on Heather, Keira had overslept. Maybe because of how good it had felt to have Roman in the bed next to her.

He hadn't been there when she woke up, but the note he'd left lying on the pillow had made up for it.

Trust me when I say there's nowhere else I'd rather be than right here with you.

She only felt like a little bit of an idiot that she folded the note and put it in her pocket so she could carry it around with her all day.

She'd been so thankful to have Roman here last night. She didn't know how Spike had found Heather or gotten in, but she knew for sure that it would've been a much different situation if not for Roman's presence.

After Keira made a call this morning and Brandon had assured her that Spike was on his way to jail, well and truly out of Heather's life, Keira was amazed at the difference in the other woman. Heather looked like a weight, a literal weight, had been lifted off her body.

Heather had smiled more this morning than in the entire five months she'd been here. Keira hadn't known how worried Heather had been that Spike would find her and baby Rachel. She hadn't asked if Spike was the baby's father because it didn't matter.

Rachel was Heather's. And now no one was ever going to try to hurt either of them again.

Largely thanks to Roman.

Gratitude hadn't been the reason Keira had allowed him into her bed. She wanted him there, and felt she'd been stupid to keep him out of it for this long, anyway. She couldn't deny to herself any longer how important Roman was becoming to her.

Not just because of the security he provided for both Fresh Starts and against Freihof, but to her personally. How he made her laugh. How he always seemed to have something interesting to talk about.

Most of all, how he cared. About her. About the baby.

How had he come to mean so much to her in this short amount of time?

Keira didn't know, but she was no longer terrified of the prospect of having him in her life. Maybe she'd blown the entire thing about his family out of proportion.

She held onto that line of thinking right up until her eleven o'clock appointment walked through the door.

Maureen Weber Donovan. Roman's mother.

The salon was already pretty chaotic. The glass repair team, fixing the window where Spike had thrown the rock, had left only a few minutes ago.

Keira was running a little bit behind schedule because of oversleeping and, damn it all, hadn't had time to put on much makeup or do much styling of her own hair.

Definitely not the way she would've chosen to face down Maureen Donovan.

When Keira saw the woman walk through the door, glancing around with one perfectly manicured eyebrow raised as if she was afraid to get too close or to touch anything, Keira rushed over to Annabel at the computer.

"Can you pull up the name of my eleven o'clock appointment?" she asked quietly.

Annabel gave her an odd look but did as she asked. "Maureen. New client. Wants a wash and style." She pointed toward the door. "I'm assuming that's her over there."

Keira nodded slowly. "It is. Ugh. I'm running a little behind, and I look terrible."

"Since when do you care how you look just to style hair all day?" Annabel laughed.

Keira tried to smile. "You're right. Can you just offer her a cup of coffee or water or something? I'll be right there."

She forced herself not to glance in Maureen's direction as she finished the hairstyle she was working on. Why was the woman here? She had to have known this was Keira's salon, right?

She finished as quickly as she could without sacrificing quality, and thanked her current client. Then there was no more avoiding it; she had to go see Maureen. Trying to calm the nerves in her stomach, she walked over to where the woman was sitting in the waiting area.

"Maureen, so sorry I was running late. I had no idea it was you who was my eleven o'clock appointment."

The older woman gave her what could only be called a condescending smile as they walked together to the salon chair.

"I just thought I would come see where my son has been spending so much time."

Keira got a whiff of Maureen's perfume and took a slight step away. It wasn't that the other woman had too much of it on—she would certainly never make that mistake—but the scent wasn't appealing to Keira.

"Roman isn't here right now. He was called back to Omega Sector."

"I see." Maureen's lips pressed together.

Keira wasn't certain if Maureen was irritated at the mention of Omega Sector or just found being here distasteful in general.

Keira straightened her back. It better not be because of Fresh Starts. Yes, the salon was a little disorganized right now because of all the action in the last twenty-four hours, but Keira was very proud of her place of business.

"What can I do for you today?" She met Maureen's eyes in the mirror. "A cut? Color?"

Maureen actually laughed out loud. "Oh no, dear. Just a style. That's all."

The answer left no doubt that the other woman didn't trust Keira to do anything permanent to her hair.

Keira didn't let her irritation show as she breathed through her mouth, not wanting to smell any more of Maureen's perfume. The expensive brand had never bothered her before, but it was now. "Let's get you over to the washing station then."

Keira's stomach was feeling pretty upset by the time she had walked Maureen just the short distance to the sink. Annabel saw her face and asked, "Hey, are you okay?"

Keira nodded, but her stomach was beginning to riot even more.

"Why don't you let me do this wash? I don't mind. Grab a cracker or something if you're not feeling well."

Maureen was watching the entire conversation with narrowed eyes. But there was nothing Keira could do. The perfume was making her sick. She slapped her hand over her mouth and made a dash for her office, barely making it to the trash can before she lost the contents of her stomach.

Damn it, had she just thrown up in front of Roman's mother?

At least she felt better now. Keira tied the trash bag off tightly, and without looking at either Annabel or Maureen, walked it outside to the Dumpster. The cold air helped clear her head and settle her stomach.

When she walked back in, Annabel had finished the wash and Maureen was back in the salon chair.

"Are you sick, dear? Perhaps you shouldn't be working if you are ill," Maureen said.

Annabel smiled over at Keira. "You look much better now. Sometimes you just have to reset your system."

Keira knew what was about to happen, what Annabel was about to do, but she couldn't figure out how to stop it.

Her assistant turned to Maureen. "Don't worry, Keira won't get you sick. I don't think pregnancy is contagious."

Annabel giggled and walked back toward the reception area, completely unaware of the bomb she'd just dropped.

Keira was left looking at Maureen in the mirror. She took out a hair dryer to dry her hair, and also to give them both some time to collect their thoughts.

But when she turned it off a few minutes later the silence was still thick with tension between them.

"Pregnant? I assume the child is my son's, considering how much time he's been spending here."

Keira got out a small curling iron and began styling Maureen's short hair. "Yes, the baby is Roman's, but that's really between us."

"Surely, given the circumstances, you would be willing to submit to a paternity test once the child is born, to make sure the baby is Roman's."

Keira's eyes met hers in the mirror again. "Exactly what circumstances are you referring to, Maureen?"

The older woman didn't flinch. "I assume the financial status of both of you hasn't changed since our conversation at the country club. To put it bluntly, Roman's family has a great deal of money, and you don't."

Keira resisted the urge to "accidentally" burn Maureen with the curling iron.

"I wasn't interested in your son's money two months ago and I'm not interested in his money now."

"Then perhaps you're thinking you would get a marriage proposal out of this? I can assure you that is not going to happen."

Keira was about to reassure the other woman that marriage was the last thing on her mind, but Maureen continued without letting her speak. "I know Roman works for that law enforcement agency right now." Her tone dripped with derision at the words *law enforcement*. "But I have no doubt he will one day be interested in at least state-level politics, like his father, if not more.

"You can certainly understand," Maureen continued, "that an ex-exotic dancer and hairstylist would not be the correct marital choice for someone like Roman."

"I can assure you I have no interest in marrying anyone. Roman included."

"Somehow I doubt that."

Keira turned off the curling iron and placed it on the workstation. "I think you better leave, Maureen. What's between Roman and me is just that—between us."

She didn't move from the chair. "I'm not trying to offend you, Keira. Truly. You just have to understand that some men are made for greatness, and I believe Roman is one of those. If you truly care for him you would just get out of his way."

Keira didn't respond. Just unwrapped the cape from around Maureen's neck.

"Keira, I am nothing if not a practical woman. I don't expect for you to leave the situation completely empty-handed. I'm willing to write you a check right now for you to take care of this pregnancy problem. You don't have to tell Roman the truth. You could just say you lost the baby. Look at you—you're not even showing yet."

Keira couldn't believe what she was hearing.

"And I could buy the salon from you outright. Name any price within reason and I'll make sure you get it. You could start a new salon, a bigger one, in a bigger town in a different state. Maybe one on the East Coast."

Keira just stared at her. "You need to leave, Maureen."

Roman's mother finally stood. "I'll give you a chance to think about my offer. Believe me, it is the best one you're going to get." She turned and faced Keira. "I know my son. He may think he has feelings for you now, but they are nothing he won't get over. Roman has a great many talents, but his strengths have never been in looking at the big picture. He doesn't see what being attached to you permanently would do to him in the future." Her eyes narrowed. "But I do. Again, nothing against you personally. It's just some people are not a good fit."

Maureen turned toward the door and took a few steps before pivoting back yet again. "I know you find what I'm saying right now offensive. You wouldn't be human if you didn't. But you're obviously a businesswoman, so I hope you will seriously consider my offer." She edged slightly closer. "If you care for my son, you'll do the right thing and remove yourself from his life. In the long run, it's best for both of you."

Keira watched as Maureen turned and walked over to Annabel, paid for the hairstyle, and briskly exited.

Annabel rushed to Keira. "Are you sure you're feeling all right? To be honest, that wasn't the best styling job you've ever done."

Considering the woman had asked her to get an abortion and move out of the state in the middle of said styling job, Keira didn't think it was that bad.

"Actually, I'm really not feeling very well. Can you cover the other appointments or reschedule them?"

Now Annabel looked truly concerned. "Yeah, sure. You just go rest."

"Thanks, Annabel."

Keira took off her smock, hung it on a peg and went up to her apartment, feeling more exhausted than she had in…forever. She stuffed her hands in her pockets and felt Roman's note in one.

Trust me when I say there's nowhere else I'd rather be than right here with you.

Keira crumpled it up and threw it away.

Chapter Nineteen

Roman sat in Steve Drackett's office along with Derek and Brandon a few hours later. The meeting was being kept as small as possible, since they didn't know who the traitor inside Omega was.

To think that it could be someone they worked with every day sickened them all. But there could be no doubt it was someone with true inside information.

Roman and Derek had been at the hospital a good chunk of the afternoon. Lillian had made it out of surgery and the doctors were optimistic in their prognosis of her recovery. But Liam hadn't awakened yet.

The nerve agent used by Freihof to lace the explosives was a version of tabun, not the most lethal chemical weapon, but certainly deadly. Despite the antidotes and drug regimens they were giving Liam, the doctors weren't sure if he would ever be functional again.

Seeing the worry on Liam's wife's face was

hard to stomach. Even worse was watching Vanessa try to explain it to Tallinn, their nine-year-old daughter, whom they'd adopted last year. Tallinn was particularly close with Liam, since he'd been the one to rescue her and her friends from a trafficking ring. As they paced the room, both Vanessa and Tallinn held one of the twins Vanessa had given birth to a few months ago.

When Roman and Derek had left the hospital, the doctors were calling it too soon to tell.

Steve walked in with a man Roman hadn't seen before. "Gentlemen, this is Cain Bennett. He's the assistant director of the Protection Division of Omega, offices of which are located in Atlanta. Cain, I think you know Brandon Han. This is Derek Waterman, leader of the SWAT team, and Roman Weber, SWAT team member."

They all shook hands and took seats around the table.

Steve hit a buzzer on his desk. "Cynthia, could you please send in Sydney."

A few moments later the same computer tech who had explained to Keira how her phone had been hacked walked in. She didn't look any more comfortable now than she had two weeks ago.

"When Sydney heard about the leak in information, she started digging through the electronic archives to see what she could find out." Steve turned to her and gestured for her to continue.

Sydney took a deep breath in and out, then began. "The call from Agent Han, after he'd questioned Spike, came in this morning at 9:32 a.m. If I'm not mistaken, the SWAT team breached Damien Freihof's town house at 10:50 a.m."

Derek nodded. "Yes, that's correct. We were on-site probably fifteen to seventeen minutes before that, but the other town houses had to be cleared."

"We don't think Freihof was clued in by the team clearing the town houses," Roman interjected. "We had an agent on the roof watching the back door, and uniformed officers at the front. But Freihof left in a hurry. He still had a pan on the stove, egg still in it, when we breached. That's how I know he was definitely tipped off by someone."

Sydney nodded. "There was a relatively small window between when Agent Han's call came in and when the SWAT team rolled out. I searched through all outgoing transmissions during that time. I found this." She handed out printed copies of a list of electronic transmissions during the time in question.

"It was pretty tedious, but I was able to eliminate all of the transmissions as going to acceptable locations except for the highlighted one. It was encrypted, and it was sent to a location matching the general vicinity of Freihof's town house."

"That's our mole," Brandon said. Everyone else nodded. "Can you tell where it came from?"

Sydney looked pained. "No, I'm so sorry. Whoever sent it knew what they were doing. As a matter fact, I have no doubt that, given the complexity of the encryption and the manner in which it was sent, whoever did it has probably gone back and erased the record of the transmission." She turned toward Steve, her shoulders slumped. "This person is better than me."

Steve shook his head. "You moved quickly and got the proof we needed that there is a traitor inside Omega Sector, so don't be too quick to discredit yourself."

"I'm just sorry I can't do more."

Steve gave her shoulder a friendly pat. "You've done a lot. We'll take it from here for now. I don't need to tell you that the information you brought to us needs to stay in this room. Until we figure out a plan, we can't tip off whoever is behind this."

Sydney nodded and Steve led her out of the office, then came back and sat down again. Derek jumped up and began pacing.

"Okay, so we have confirmation that there's a mole and he or she is feeding info to Freihof,"

Derek said, frustration clear in his tone. "But that doesn't get us any closer to catching him. Damn it, Steve, I have two of my team members in the hospital. We almost lost Roman a couple of months ago."

"That's what Cain is here for." Steve gestured to the man, who had sat silently through Sydney's entire report. Roman realized it was because the information was not new to Cain Bennett.

"Right now, our biggest problem is knowing who we can trust," Steve continued. "Besides the people sitting in this office and a few select others, there's no one I trust one hundred percent. All we know is that the traitor is definitely from this office and that he or she has a technical savviness that goes beyond what Sydney is capable of."

"Not to be an ass," Roman said, "but are we sure Sydney is not our mole?"

Steve nodded. "She was the first one I checked out. Very thoroughly. Plus she's only been here a month, and we had the traitor in place before that."

There wasn't much arguing with that logic.

Brandon looked at Cain. "So you have the technological ability to figure out who this mole is?"

Cain shook his head and spoke for the first time. "Not me. But I know someone who does. She and I will be working off-site so as not to cause the mole to panic and go to ground."

Cain Bennett's eyes were hard. Roman had no doubt the man took every aspect of his job seriously.

Good. Because Omega couldn't continue to take hits like they had been.

"Do you have a backup plan in case Hayley Green is unavailable?" Steve asked. "Or if she just refuses to have anything to do with you, since, you know, you sent her to prison?"

Cain crossed his arms over his chest, one eyebrow raised. "Don't worry about Hayley Green. I'll handle her. When she finds out that she could stop someone like Damien Freihof, she'll help us."

If Cain had put her in jail, Roman wasn't so sure. But he didn't say anything.

"Like I told Sydney, we need to keep this to the smallest circle possible. If the mole gets wind that we're onto him and have a way of closing in, we may lose him—or her—for good." Steve stood. "If we get anything usable back from Freihof's town house, I'll be sure to let you know. Until then, unfortunately, we're back to the waiting game."

ROMAN WAS MORE than ready to get back to the salon and Keira by later that afternoon. He'd stopped at the hospital on his way, but there was little change in Liam's status. Lillian's rage at being trapped in a hospital bed had her ready to kill everyone within a fifty-mile radius, so Roman didn't stay there long, either.

At Fresh Starts, he checked in with the agent who had been watching over the salon and Keira while he'd been gone. There seemed to be nothing to report except that Keira had gotten a little ill, and had canceled some of her afternoon appointments.

When Roman found Keira up in her apartment, she seemed to be fine. If fine could be considered reorganizing your closet rather than working. She was muttering to herself as she changed the arrangement of her shoes.

"Hi," he said from the doorway of the large closet. "What are you doing in there?"

She didn't look at him, didn't turn, didn't smile. "I'm going to need room for baby stuff. I might even need to turn this entire closet into a small baby's room."

Keira's voice sounded different. Strange. Not the normal confident tone she usually spoke with.

"Okay. But I think we've got a little bit of time. You don't necessarily have to do it all today, since the baby's not coming for another six or seven months." Roman kept his own tone as soothing as he could make it.

"I need to get started. It's always better to be prepared than to get caught unawares."

She still hadn't looked at him.

"The agent downstairs said you got a little sick today. Are you feeling better? Do you want me to take you to the doctor?"

She put down the shoes she had in her hand and turned to him for just a second, before quickly turning back around. "No, I'm okay. That was just a reaction to…a client's perfume."

He supposed stuff like that was to be expected, and wished he knew more about pregnancy.

"Do you want me to make us some dinner? I'm not much of a cook but I could do omelets. Or if that's not appealing, I'll certainly order us something."

"I've already eaten," she muttered, stacking another pair of shoes.

Okay. Obviously, something wasn't going right here. He tried a different track. "How's Heather today? The DEA arrested Spike, and he'll be going to jail for a long time. Won't be bothering her again."

Keira nodded. "It's amazing the difference in her. She's almost a completely different person, knowing she doesn't have to deal with him ever again, or at least for a really long time."

All right, Heather was fine, so that wasn't what was bothering Keira.

"I left you a note this morning. I didn't want you to think I just ran off. I tried to wake you up but you weren't having any of it."

She turned to him slightly now. "Yeah, I saw it. Thanks."

He sat there watching her for a couple minutes when she didn't say anything else. It didn't take long to realize she was taking the same four pairs of shoes and just moving them from place to place.

What exactly was going on here?

"You know, I was thinking that maybe instead of you making this closet a baby room, maybe we could knock out the south wall and connect your apartment to the one next to it. It would give us more space."

The thought had come to Roman a few days ago. He had realized that Keira was never going to leave Fresh Starts. This was her heart's work. If Roman wanted to be in her life on a permanent basis, he was going to have to be a part of Fresh Starts and its mission, as well.

Her apartment really wasn't big enough for a family, but if they knocked out the wall into the apartment next door they could have a reasonably sized three-bedroom living space, with two bathrooms.

Roman planned to be a part of Keira's and the baby's life in whatever way he could.

"But that would be too much space for me, even with the baby."

"But it wouldn't be too much space for the three of us."

Now she turned around and looked at him. She stood and he moved forward to help her, but she held her hand out to ward him off. Roman stopped.

"You know I'll never try to keep you from the baby," she said. "But we don't have to be a traditional family."

"What if I want to be a traditional family?"

"To be honest, I don't know if I even have that in me. Not to mention, what about your political aspirations? I'm pretty sure the baby and I don't fall into those."

"Any political aspirations I have damn well better include you and the baby, because you're a part of me now."

She brushed past him as she left the closet. "You think that now, but you're not really considering the future. You're not good at looking at the big picture."

Roman's eyes narrowed as it suddenly all made sense to him. "You talked to my mother today."

Keira rubbed her forearms. "It doesn't matter. What matters is that the baby and I would be holding you back from the future you want. Politics, like your father."

Roman had no doubt she'd spoken with his mother now. He'd heard the "politics like your father" speech from Maureen so many times he knew it by heart.

"Do I get a say in all this? Do I get a say in what my future will hold? Or does my mother get to decide for me?"

Keira stopped, studying him. Now he was finally reaching her. Keira had fought for her independence and didn't like the thought of anyone making decisions for someone else.

She looked at him fully for the first time, her big brown eyes intense. "Of course you do. But I just don't want to trap you, to keep you from the future you might not want right now, but will in the future."

He started to argue again, but she held out her hand so she could continue. "I'm never going to get married, Roman. I just want to make sure you understand. I cannot put myself through that again."

He ignored the tightness in his chest. "I know you feel that way right now, but maybe your views will change."

"Do you know what I picture when I think of marriage? My jaw being broken in two places, and the two cracked ribs that made me feel like I couldn't breathe for over a month and a half. I can literally feel those pains when I think of intertwining my life in a permanent fashion with someone else's."

Roman felt like he'd been punched in the gut, but he didn't let it show. "Fine, then we won't get married. But that doesn't mean I don't want to be a permanent part of your and the baby's life."

"Don't you see? By doing that you would ruin any chance you have of ever running for political office."

"Fine. Then I won't ever run for political office. That was my mother's dream, not mine."

The sadness in Keira's eyes clutched at his heart. "Maybe not your dream, but you knew it was part of your destiny."

Roman scrubbed a hand over his face. He couldn't argue with that, not without lying. That was exactly how he thought of it—that running for office one day would be a part of his destiny. But looking at Keira now, he realized that wasn't true anymore.

"Maybe at one time." He took a step closer to her. "Especially when my father was alive. But I've come to realize what my mother never has, and that is that my father was about doing *good,* not about being a politician. He wanted to help people."

"You want to help people, too. I know it."

"Yes, but running for office isn't the only way to do that. As a matter fact, I'm not sure it's even the *best* way to do that. Maybe staying in Omega

Sector is the best way. Maybe helping you run the shelter is the best way."

He took the final couple of steps between them and pulled her into his arms, desperately relieved when she didn't pull away.

"There's a lot of unknowns out there right now. Let's just take it one day at a time."

"Okay," she murmured against his chest.

Roman just held her. After everything that had happened today, he needed to be near her, to hold her against him.

They didn't say anything else for a long time. Roman realized he may have squeaked through this battle, but he was a long way from winning the war.

Chapter Twenty

"Um, Keira, I'm so sorry, but I just realized that the lady with the perfume that made you sick has an appointment ten minutes from now. So you might want to eat some crackers or something." Annabel bit her lip as she delivered the news, obviously confused.

After the terrible job Keira had done on Maureen's hair last week, she didn't blame Annabel for being confused about why the woman would ever come in again.

But Keira knew.

She grimaced. Everything had been going well between her and Roman for the last few days. Neither of them had brought up the future. There was enough to worry about now. Especially given that Roman had almost been killed again by an explosion Freihof set up.

And Roman had been right about the future, anyway. No one could choose his destiny except him. And in this day and age, if he wanted to go into politics despite not having a wife by his side, he certainly should be allowed to do that. Or, as he'd said, there were a lot of other ways to make a difference that didn't involve politics at all.

And Keira could admit she liked having him here. In her bed. Cracking jokes with her at breakfast.

"When did Maureen make this appointment?" Keira asked.

"She just called this morning. About an hour and a half ago. She's lucky we had a spot."

So Maureen had waited until Roman had been called back to Omega before making an appointment. Interesting. Keira wondered if the other woman had someone watching the salon all the time or if she just had someone watching Roman.

At least today Keira wasn't so flustered and rushed. She wouldn't let Maureen pick a fight. Wouldn't let the other woman upset her.

Keira would style the woman's hair better than it had ever been styled before and then tell whoever was working reservations from now on not to allow her to make an appointment.

"She actually made an appointment for two people," Annabel continued.

Great. Probably Angela, Roman's sister.

No matter what, Keira would not get into a battle with Maureen Donovan.

But when Maureen walked through the door a

few minutes later, Keira realized she'd underestimated the woman as an opponent.

Maureen hadn't brought her daughter with her for the other appointment. She had brought Bridgette Cunningham.

Keira's ex-mother-in-law.

Shock flooded Keira's system. "Bridgette?" She hadn't seen the woman since her divorce hearing, where she'd finally rid herself of Jonathan.

"That's right," Maureen said, her tone too bright. "I ran into my friend Bridgette while I was in Denver yesterday. Once I realized the connection between you two, I knew I had to invite her here for a sort of reunion."

Keira's eyes flew rapidly to the door as she tried to get her panicked breathing under control. "Jonathan?" Had Bridgette brought her son with her?

Bridgette shook her head. "No. Jonathan's not here. His father and I haven't seen him in over a year."

That made Keira feel marginally better. At least Jonathan wasn't about to burst through the door at any moment.

Maureen, completely oblivious to the tense undertones of the conversation between Keira and Bridgette, no doubt because it didn't serve her purposes, continued her monologue.

"When I found out you had been married before, I have to admit I wasn't surprised." Maureen didn't even stop to let the insult sink in before continuing. "But then I found out you were married to a *Cunningham*. A small world, isn't it?"

And by "small world" Keira assumed Maureen meant that Keira had already tried to scam her way into a rich family once and hadn't succeeded. She'd brought Bridgette here as proof that Maureen was onto Keira's schemes.

Maureen had no idea what lengths Keira had gone to to get away from this family.

"Yes, small world," Bridgette muttered.

Keira hadn't had a lot of contact with Jonathan's mother during her marriage. At least not during the abusive part. It had been his father who had always threatened her in the hospital. But Keira knew Bridgette had also known what was going on.

"Oh…" Maureen drew out the word. "I guess I didn't think this through. Didn't think that this might be awkward for both of you."

Keira knew the exact opposite to be true. Maureen had brought Bridgette here with the express intent of making things uncomfortable, or worse.

"Mother? What are you doing here?"

Keira spun toward the door at the sound of Roman's voice.

Maureen obviously wasn't expecting her son, but she recovered quickly. "Roman, darling." She crossed the few feet to him and kissed him on the cheek. "I thought you had gone into the office."

Roman's eyebrow rose. "And how would you know that, Mother?"

Maureen ignored the question completely. "I'm here to get my hair styled. And I brought my friend Bridgette Cunningham. You know the Cunninghams of Denver, don't you, darling?"

"I know of them." Roman turned to Bridgette. "It's nice to meet you, Mrs. Cunningham."

Keira glanced at Maureen as Roman shook the hand of her ex-mother-in-law. Triumph was evident in the older woman's eyes.

"It seems that our Keira and Bridgette have a tie to each other that I've just become aware of."

Roman looked at his mother. "Is that so? And what is that?"

"Keira used to be married to Bridgette's son, Jonathan."

Keira could actually see rage fill Roman as he put together these final pieces of the story of her past. She had told him about her marriage, and now he had a name to put with the villain. His eyes turned icy as he looked back at Bridgette.

Maureen misunderstood it all. "I see you're as surprised as I was to find out that Keira was married before," she said. "It's a shocking thing, I know, to think you know someone so well, only to find out you don't really know them at all."

Roman ignored his mother completely. When he slipped an arm around Keira and pulled her protectively to his side, Maureen's eyes narrowed. She became aware that his anger was directed at Bridgette, not Keira.

"Roman, certainly you don't think that Bridgette would lie about something like this? Ask Keira yourself if you don't believe she was married before."

"I knew Keira was married before, Mother. What I didn't know was to whom." He hadn't known because Keira had asked him to leave the past behind them, and Keira appreciated that he'd done so.

Realizing her mistake, Maureen changed the track of her argument instantly. "Well, good. I'm glad Keira told you. But you have to admit it's a very odd coincidence that Keira has attached herself to another wealthy family, after a marriage to the son of the first wealthy family didn't work out."

If Maureen had said Keira was a scheming, money-hungry bitch her intent couldn't have been more plain.

"I know exactly why Keira got a divorce from Jonathan Cunningham." Roman's eyes never left Bridgette's. The older woman flinched.

"It's time for you to leave," he said to her.

"You're being terribly rude, Roman," Maureen

protested. "I brought Bridgette here so that you could see the truth about Keira. Not so that you could be rude to one of my friends."

"If the Cunninghams are your friends, Mother, then I can honestly say that I don't know if I can be a part of our family anymore."

"What are you talking about?"

"I'm talking about the fact that you have no idea what the Cunninghams are evidently capable of." He gestured toward Bridgette with the arm that wasn't wrapped around Keira, then turned to the woman again. "Like I said, it is time for you to leave. Right now."

Maureen, becoming aware she was losing a much bigger battle, remained quiet.

Bridgette just nodded. She didn't try to defend herself or her family in any way. "I will leave. I will never come back to this place or bother Keira again. But can I have just one moment with her alone?"

Keira could feel Roman tense even more. She reached over and touched his arm. It was nice having someone fight for her for a change, but she was strong enough to handle this.

"It's okay," she whispered.

"You don't have to talk to her if you don't want to." He pulled her closer and kissed her temple as he muttered the words.

"I'll be all right." Just knowing he was nearby helped. "I'll give her three minutes."

"Does someone want to tell me what in the world is going on here?" Maureen's voice seemed like a loud shriek after the quietness of everyone else's words.

"You're going outside with me, Mother." He let go of Keira and walked over and took his mother's arm. "You and I have a lot to talk about, like how you're never going to set foot in this salon again, either."

Maureen sputtered about protecting the family and not tainting the Weber name as Roman dragged her out the door. He turned just before it closed behind them, and looked from Keira to Bridgette.

"Three minutes. Not one second more. I work for one of the most prestigious law enforcement agencies in the country. For whatever reason, Keira protected your son from prosecution for years. Trust me when I say I do not have that same compulsion."

Bridgette became even paler at Roman's words.

"Like I told Keira, my husband and I haven't seen Jonathan in over a year."

Roman nodded sharply, then walked out the door with Maureen. Annabel had been watching the entire scene with interest. Keira gave her friend a nod and she left the reception area, leaving Keira and Bridgette alone.

Keira crossed her arms over her chest as she looked at Bridgette. "You have three minutes."

"I just want you to know that I never really understood what Jonathan did to you. I knew he had a temper, that he had struck women in the past, but I didn't know he was *so* violent."

Keira brought her hand up to her eyes and rubbed them wearily. "You'll have to excuse me if I find that hard to believe, or at the very least, completely unacceptable to be so oblivious."

Bridgette nodded. "I don't blame you for feeling that way. It *was* unacceptable. Everything that happened to you was completely unacceptable."

"Your husband knew about it, even if you didn't. He knew about it from the very first time Jonathan put me in the hospital, if not much earlier."

If possible, Bridgette's face became even paler. "No. You must be mistaken."

Keira could feel fury pooling in her. "Your husband came to me while I lay in the hospital and told me how he would make sure the doctors' statements were changed and that I would look like the villain—unstable, alcoholic—if I tried to bring charges against Jonathan."

Bridgette didn't try to deny it, just looked at Keira with devastation in her eyes. "I didn't know he told you that. I knew my husband wanted to protect Jonathan. He's our only child."

Keira rolled her eyes. "Well, again, you'll forgive me if that doesn't quite make up for the fact that I lived for years in terror and pain before finally being able to buy my freedom with my own blood. All I ever wanted to do was get away from Jonathan once he started to hurt me. Your husband stopped me from doing that."

"I'm sorry. I'm sorry for the pain you suffered. I'm sorry that I was oblivious to it. At the time, I didn't realize how mentally ill my son was. Is." Bridgette took a step back. "Not that that changes what happened to you or makes it any more acceptable. And I'm sorry to hear that my husband was complicit in the abuse you suffered. It changes a lot of things for me."

Keira almost felt bad for the woman. But the twenty-year-old inside her who had driven across three states with broken ribs and a fractured wrist because of what this woman's son had done wouldn't allow her to.

"I won't come here again. I wouldn't have come here at all if it wasn't for Maureen and whatever sort of trouble she was trying to stir up." Bridgette nodded as if gathering her strength. "If it helps, her plan backfired. I'm glad to see you with Roman, Keira. That man obviously loves you and is never going to let anyone hurt you again."

With that, Bridgette turned and walked back out the door.

Chapter Twenty-One

Roman made sure to position himself so that he
could see inside the salon as he spoke to his mom
out in the parking lot.

"I don't know what Keira has told you about
her relationship with Jonathan, but I've known the
Cunninghams for years and I am sure Keira must
be mostly at fault for their breakup."

Roman barely listened to his mother as he
watched to make sure Bridgette wasn't doing or
saying anything to upset Keira.

"Mother, I hope to God you didn't know what
was happening in Jonathan and Keira's marriage."

Maureen gave an exasperated sigh. "Of course
not. I hardly even know Jonathan. The only thing
I remember was that the marriage was a bit of
a scandal because the son refused to have a big
wedding."

Roman wondered if the abuse had begun even
before the marriage had. Keira had been alone and

unprotected, with no parents to give her advice, or for her to turn to if she was in trouble.

"But Roman, you have to admit it's quite suspicious that Keira was married to Jonathan Cunningham and now is interested in you. She's just using you, can't you see that?"

All Roman could see was that Keira was listening to a woman who had begged for an audience, even though Keira didn't owe her a thing. Owed her less than nothing.

"She's not using me."

"I know about the baby. If she's really even pregnant." Maureen began to pace back and forth. "Don't think that I'm not going to demand a paternity test."

Roman whipped his head around to stare at his mother. "You will do no such thing."

She was obviously flustered by his tone. He couldn't blame her. He'd probably never spoken that way to her in his entire life. He'd coddled his mother and protected her after his father's death. Allowed her to feel like she had some control over his life and plans in order to give her something to live for. But she didn't need that anymore and it was time Maureen realized exactly where she stood.

Roman loved his mother, but there was no way in hell he was going to allow her to damage his relationship with Keira.

"Roman, surely you can see she is trying to trap you. She undoubtedly did it with Jonathan Cunningham. That didn't work out the way she planned, and now she's moved on to you."

His mother loved him, Roman knew. And she was stubborn. And she wanted to protect Roman's father's legacy and memory more than anything in the world.

But he was finished hearing her disparage Keira. For good.

Roman pulled out his phone. His mother probably would not accept the words, but she would not be able to deny the images. The pictures Roman had found from Keira's hospital stay six years ago. Not just one, but *multiple* hospital stays.

Keira had made him promise not to look into her ex-husband, and he'd kept that promise. But Roman had needed to know exactly what had been done to her.

"This is the reason Keira's marriage with Jonathan Cunningham fell apart." Roman flipped his phone around so that his mother was confronted with the image on the screen.

"And this is another reason." He flipped to another picture. "And here's another. I would say those were plenty of reasons to petition for divorce, wouldn't you?"

Maureen blanched. "Jonathan Cunningham did that to her?"

"Yes, Mother. Look at Bridgette in there. She didn't hold any ill will against Keira, because she knew what Jonathan did to her."

Maureen's eyes flew to the salon. "I had no idea."

Bridgette walked out of the building. She gave a small wave to Maureen, but didn't come over to talk, just walked to her car and left.

Roman watched her go. "I don't know if Bridgette Cunningham knew about the abuse, but I know her husband did. He threatened Keira, Mom. Threatened to use the Cunningham name and power if she tried to press charges or to leave Jonathan."

Maureen brought her hands up to her face. "Oh, my God."

Roman knew he could probably stop there, but he had to make Maureen understand the full extent of it.

"Keira owns this salon free and clear, Mom. She doesn't need me to support her financially. Keira isn't after my money. Or my name. Or the clout it carries. The opposite, actually."

"Roman…"

"If I didn't have any money, if she didn't see me as having political aspirations, it would probably be much easier to get her to agree to be in my life permanently."

Roman shook his head, looking toward Fresh

Starts. "She's an amazing woman. Has a strength I don't know that I'll ever have. But that strength was bought at a price. And she doesn't know if she'll ever be able to permanently tie herself to someone else again."

"How could anyone not want to tie themselves to you?" The disbelief was clear in his mother's tone.

"She's definitely not trying to trap me. That's what I want you to understand. If anything, I'm trying to trap her. I want her and the baby in my life forever. And however long it takes for me to convince her of that, to convince her she means everything to me and that I'm never going to hurt her..." Roman shrugged. "I don't know if I'll ever be able to convince her, but I'll spend my life trying."

Maureen gave a shuddery sigh. "I had no idea you felt that way. That this relationship, even with the baby, was so important to you." She wrung her hands. "I did a bad thing last week, Roman. I offered to give her money if she left."

A muscle in Roman's jaw twitched. "I figured it was something like that. But Mother, you're going to have to accept that I choose Keira. And hopefully, she'll choose me back."

Maureen took a step closer, her arm reaching toward him before dropping to her side. "But you've always wanted to run for office, like your father. I don't know if she's a good fit for you."

Roman shook his head. "No, Mother, I wanted to *help* like Dad did. That's why Dad was in politics, because he wanted to be able to make the world a better place."

His mother put her hands on his arms. "Yes. Exactly. And you could do the same good, just like him. But Keira Spencer is not the right woman to be standing next to you as you do that. She doesn't strike me as the type of person who puts others before herself. As someone who wants to help. Not that I blame her for being self-sufficient or protecting herself. Especially after what you said happened with Jonathan."

Roman took his mother's hands off his arms and turned her so she was standing beside him, facing the salon. "What do you see there, Mom?"

"Roman..."

"Humor me, Mother. What do you see when you look at the building in front of you?"

Maureen gave an exasperated sigh. "I see a decent salon in a relatively good section of town. Probably a solid business choice." She turned to Roman. "But all this proves is that she has a sufficient business head on her shoulders. That's not surprising to me."

"She owns the whole building, Mom. Paid for it free and clear with some money her parents left for her when she turned twenty-five. Not just the bottom section housing the salon, but the six apartments above it."

Maureen shrugged. "Tax-wise, that probably wasn't the best move, to buy it outright. But is she planning on using the apartments for further income? Depending on what shape they are in that could be a good financial investment."

One thing Roman loved about his mother was her business savvy. She could appreciate a shrewd corporate move better than most. Had an eye for it. It had been what made her such a good partner to his father.

"Those apartments on top of the salon? Keira uses them as a shelter for women who have been trafficked or are running from an abusive situation. Keira doesn't charge the women anything to stay here, and then she teaches them a skill, either with hairdressing or some other type of cosmetology trade, so they have a means of supporting themselves."

He watched his mother stare at the building. "Fresh Starts."

"Exactly. It's not just about someone getting a nice haircut."

"I had no idea."

"There is more to Keira than meets the eye. And there are more ways that I can help, that I can give back to society, than by running for office. That may have been the plan once, but I don't know that it is anymore."

"Then what is the plan?"

"Keira is the plan. Keira and the baby."

"I WANT TO kill her right now."

Damien Freihof sat back easily in the passenger side of the car in the back of the parking lot, pointed toward Fresh Starts salon. Jonathan Cunningham sat in the driver's seat.

The man had already tried to harm Keira twice, both off Damien's schedule. Once during the blizzard and once after Damien had first contacted him and Jonathan had decided to sneak around the salon, where Keira had almost caught him.

Damien needed to get him back on track. "I would not suggest that, given that Roman Weber, one of the Omega SWAT team members, is standing directly outside her front door."

"I'll kill him, too. He's the one who's been sleeping with her."

Damien had to keep Jonathan under control. The man was just disturbed enough, just idiotic enough, to think he could take on Roman and win.

But telling him that outright wasn't going to do much good. Jonathan lived in his own fantasy world. If Damien wanted to talk him into doing something, he had to work within that fantasy.

"I have no doubt you could take him." Lie. "But

don't you think it's better to wait? To make your wife suffer? The way you've suffered. If you just go in there with a gun and shoot them both, then how will she really suffer?"

Jonathan's eyes narrowed as he stared at the salon. "I guess you're right. Keira deserves to suffer. I was always so good to her, then she left me."

Damien nodded. "Yes, some women just don't appreciate it when they have it good."

Actually, Damien did understand that a little bit. His wife, Natalie, had never appreciated how good her life was with him. And then, before Damien could really prove it to her, Omega Sector had taken her away from him.

"And my mom was in there. I wouldn't want to accidentally hurt her."

Damien had been surprised to see Bridgette Cunningham at the salon, brought in by Maureen Donovan. But ultimately, it didn't really matter. Let their own personal drama play out however they wanted it to. Damien just needed to lie low for a few days.

They had blown up his house.

If Mr. Fawkes hadn't notified him that the SWAT team was on their way, they would've caught him.

Such a close call made Damien very angry.

Ended up that Spike guy was a little bit smarter than Damien had given him credit for. He had sent one of his men to follow Damien and then used that information to cut a deal with law enforcement.

Spike didn't know that the medicine he would be receiving later this afternoon in the hospital was laced with tetrodotoxin. Damien wouldn't have to worry about Spike following him anymore. And the woman who lived with Keira in the apartments over the salon wouldn't have to worry about Spike bothering her ever again. Damien didn't take well to people who thought they could betray him.

Fortunately, the explosives at his house had worked the way they should, protecting Damien's secrets from Omega. Sadly, no one on the SWAT team was killed, but Damien understood there were some pretty severe injuries.

Good. Mr. Fawkes's plan to take down all of Omega and reset the law enforcement establishment as a whole, with some other very well placed explosives, was almost ready to go.

Damien just had to keep Omega focused on him a few more weeks.

Or, more specifically, get people like Jonathan Cunningham to do the dirty work for him. Omega wouldn't know who exactly they were chasing.

It was all coming together. Time to stop toying around with them. He'd enjoyed killing Grace Parker, but he was growing tired of the game. He was ready to work with Mr. Fawkes to destroy Omega Sector for good.

Fawkes wanted to destroy Omega to change the landscape of law enforcement. To force changes at the most fundamental level. And also, Damien suspected, because Omega Sector had rejected him in some way.

Damien didn't hold the same ideological aspirations as Fawkes.

He just wanted Omega Sector to burn. The way Natalie had burned.

But right now he needed to keep Jonathan Cunningham under control, for a couple more days. Then Damien would turn the man loose to do whatever he wanted with poor Ms. Spencer. Damien and Fawkes would help Jonathan and his efforts by agitating things at Omega.

Always one of Damien's favorite pastimes.

Chapter Twenty-Two

The next few days went by without incident, from either Roman's mother or from Damien Freihof.

Omega did receive an update from the DEA that Ronald "Spike" Dunham had died in the hospital, due to a rare allergic reaction to a medication he was given. Omega had looked into it, of course, but was still waiting for results to see if Spike's death had truly been an accident.

Roman doubted it. That the man who had given them their closest lead to finding Freihof had accidentally died a couple days later? Roman didn't believe it for a second.

Defeating Freihof and capturing the mole were of critical importance. Omega couldn't keep splitting its focus the way it had been.

So when Roman got the text from Steve's personal cell phone, he was ready.

I don't want to use Omega channels because of the mole. Confirmed spotting Freihof.

The next message contained an address only a couple miles from the salon. Roman was already running up the stairs to Keira's apartment for his backup sidearms.

You're closest. I'm calling local PD for support, but you're most likely to catch him. I'll send someone to the salon for protection detail.

Wait for backup if you can. Be careful. You know Freihof is dangerous.

Yeah, Roman had scars all over his shoulder and back as proof. Two other Omega Sector agents were in the hospital as testament to how dangerous Freihof was.

Roman wouldn't underestimate him. But neither was he going to miss a chance to catch him just because he didn't have backup.

Keira was in the middle of teaching Heather a new styling skill when Roman came back down through the salon. She took one look at his face in the mirror and excused herself.

He pulled her into her office.

"What? What happened?"

"We have a confirmed sighting of Freihof a couple of miles from here. I'm the closest Omega agent to the scene."

Keira nodded. "Then go get him. But be careful." She reached out and fisted her hand in his shirt, pulling him closer. "You be careful," she said again.

Roman nodded. He wasn't worried about his safety. "Steve is sending someone else here to make sure you guys are safe. Don't go anywhere until the agent gets here."

She shook her head. "I won't. Don't worry about me—I've got nowhere to go. You focus on what you need to do."

He reached out and placed his hands on her cheeks, then threaded his fingers into her hair and pulled her up against him. He felt her arms wrap around his waist as his lips covered hers.

The kiss was brief, but expressed everything they couldn't say to each other right now. And not just because he had to go.

"Soon," he said against her lips. "Soon."

He wasn't sure if he meant Freihof would be caught soon or the two of them would be together soon. It didn't matter.

"Yes."

He kissed her one more time and then turned and ran out the door without looking back. This was the chance. Hopefully, Freihof didn't know he had been spotted.

The address Steve had sent him was one of the larger pawnshops in town. Perhaps Freihof was planning to purchase a new weapon, or needed some money after his home was destroyed.

Roman didn't care why the man was here, he just wanted to catch him.

The police backup hadn't arrived when Roman pulled up at the door. Roman decided he couldn't wait. The element of surprise was the biggest factor in his favor right now.

He walked in the door casually, as if he was a customer, with his Glock hidden behind his leg, hoping not to draw any undue attention to himself in case Freihof was just inside the main room.

He immediately took stock of his surroundings. A young couple stood over in the corner, looking at jewelry. An older man was looking at the shop's collection of rifles with a store associate. And a couple kids in their teens, probably skipping school, were looking through DVDs and video games.

Roman didn't think the older man could be Freihof, but given his ability to disguise himself, Roman wasn't willing to take the chance.

He walked over to where the employee was showing the older man the guns. Roman pulled out his badge with one hand, keeping his sidearm low but ready. He watched as the employee's eyes grew wide.

"I'm a federal officer. I need you to put your hands on the counter please, sir."

The older man glanced at Roman with one eyebrow raised, but did as he asked. "I'm buying this gun legally, son. Have gone through more than the two-day waiting period."

Looking at him more closely, Roman realized there was no way this could be a disguise. But he had to try.

"Sir, if you will pardon me for just a moment…" Roman reached up and grabbed some short strands of hair at the back of the older man's skull, what little of it there was, and tugged.

Nothing happened. This wasn't a wig. This wasn't a disguise. This wasn't Freihof.

"You pulling my hair for a reason, son?" the old man asked.

Roman offered his apology and then turned to the employee, a much younger man, who was still looking on in surprise. "Anybody in the rear of the store?"

The guy shook his head. "Um, I'm pretty sure my boss went to the bank. The assistant manager, his wife, might be in the office."

"Anybody else? A customer? Did you see anybody head back there who shouldn't be there?"

The kid wouldn't stop shaking his head. "No. No. It's been a pretty slow day. I haven't seen anybody go back there. Almost everything we have to sell is out here, anyway."

Roman glanced out the window, hoping to

see his police backup, but there was nothing. He looked more thoroughly at the other people in the room. Based on height and weight and gender, there was no way any of them could be Freihof, even if he was disguising himself.

He held out his badge again. "I need everyone to exit this building please." He turned to the employee, who had Tyrese printed on his name tag. "Tyrese, can you give me a brief layout of the rooms in the back. We've got a situation here that could possibly be dangerous."

Now Tyrese's head went from vigorous shaking to vigorous nodding. "Yeah, man." He pointed toward the rear door. "When you first enter the hallway, there's a bathroom on the left. The next door, on the right, is the manager's office."

"Any other rooms back there?"

"Just a small closet where we keep cleaning supplies and stuff. My boss has a warehouse where he keeps all the other merchandise, so none of that is on-site."

Roman began walking toward the door. "Is there a back door leading outside? Do any of the offices or closets have windows?"

"There's a door at the end of the hall that leads to the back parking lot. But there aren't any windows."

Roman nodded. "Tyrese, get these people out front. And wait for the police to arrive."

Roman kept his weapon drawn as he walked into the hallway.

He cleared the bathroom first, pushing the door open. There was nowhere to hide in here. He pulled the door closed behind him when he left.

Roman glanced at the door that led out to the parking lot. It didn't look like it had been used recently or propped open. He wished he had more information about the people who owned this pawnshop. Could they perhaps be working with Freihof in some way? Some of the "partners" he'd convinced to go after someone in or connected to Omega Sector?

Roman didn't like going into a situation blind without backup, but he didn't have any choice. He stood in front of the office door, counted from three, then kicked the door in, automatically dropping low in case someone fired from inside.

The only person in the office was an older woman standing at a filing cabinet. Upon seeing Roman and his gun, she immediately backed up against the wall, her arms raised in front of her.

"We don't have any money in here. All the cash is in the register in the front or goes straight to the bank."

Roman reached for his badge and showed it to her. "I'm a federal agent. Has anybody been back in this office with you for the last few minutes? Have you seen anyone else around here?"

The woman didn't lower her hands, since Roman didn't lower his gun. She shook her head. "Just my husband. He's taking a deposit to the bank."

Damn it. Roman must have missed Freihof. Gotten here too late.

His phone buzzed in his pocket. Roman put down his weapon and picked it up, glancing at the caller ID. Steve.

"Steve, I missed him. If Freihof was here, he's not here now." Roman answered without any preamble.

"Where? At the salon? Have you seen him?"

"No. At the pawnshop. The address you sent me in your text a little while ago."

"What pawnshop? What text?"

Roman turned and walked back out into the hallway. "You didn't send me a text a few minutes ago with an address? A confirmed sighting of Freihof? Said you didn't want to use Omega channels because of the mole."

"That wasn't me, Roman. I was just calling to give you the good news that Liam has awakened."

Oh, no.

Roman began running toward the front of the store, where his vehicle was parked.

"Steve, this was a trap. I left Keira alone because I thought you were sending me here based on a sighting of Freihof."

Steve cursed under his breath. "I'll get uniforms over there right away. And some people to that pawnshop."

"I'm on my way back to the salon now. I'll touch base when I get there." Roman clicked off as he threw open his truck door.

"Hey, sir?" Tyrese rushed up to him. "Did you find the person you were looking for?"

"No. I don't think he was here at all."

"Oh, okay. Sorry, man. Look, some old dude, not the guy who was buying the gun but somebody else? Anyways, he gave me this note and said to give it to the police guy. I think that's you."

Tyrese handed him the note.

Roman opened it and read the words printed in block letters, his gut clenching as he did so.

Thanks for coming out to play, Agent Weber. But I've got other friends who want to play, too. But not with you.

Roman turned to Tyrese. "There's going to be some cops here soon to take your statement. You need to describe what the guy who gave this to you looked like, as much as possible."

Tyrese nodded again. "Sure, man. But I don't think I have to describe him. The guy knew where our security camera was. Walked right up to it, smiled and waved."

Roman didn't wait to hear any more. Freihof was toying with them once again. The only saving grace in this entire situation was that if Freihof had been here at the pawnshop, waving at the camera, then he couldn't be at Fresh Starts.

But that didn't stop Roman from gunning the engine to get back there as soon as possible.

Because in his gut he knew that Freihof had lured him out so that he could get to Keira.

Roman's fears were confirmed five minutes later when, after breaking a number of traffic laws to get back to the salon, he arrived and found Annabel in tears in front of the building. Heather stood next to her, with her arms wrapped around the hysterical woman.

He rushed up to them. "Annabel, what happened? Is Keira okay?"

"He took her, Roman. Right after you left he came storming inside the salon. He had a gun."

Just after he left? Holy God, had Freihof had Keira in the car when he stopped by the pawnshop and gave Tyrese his little note? Had she been that close and Roman didn't know it?

Fear churned like acid in his gut.

"She wasn't going to go with him. I could tell," Annabel said, crying again. "Even if he had a gun pointed at her she wasn't going to go with him."

"But then he pointed the gun at Annabel and me," Heather continued, when it seemed like Annabel wouldn't be able to get any other words out. "That man hates her, Roman. And he's not right in the head. Talking about finally having her back where she belonged."

Back where she belonged? Freihof tended to wax poetic about getting his revenge, but as far as Roman knew, he'd never really made it personal with his victims. This sounded much more personal.

He got out his phone and showed them a picture of Freihof. "Is this the guy who took her?"

They both looked at the photo and shook their head. "No," Annabel said. "That's definitely not him."

"Are you sure? Freihof is known for his disguises. Really good ones."

"No. The guy that took Keira was younger. Her age, or maybe a year or two older. Taller. More frat-boy looking."

"I heard her call him Jonathan as they stepped out the door," Annabel said. "But I don't know who Jonathan is."

Realization dawned quickly. Freihof had just used himself as bait to draw Roman away. He probably had been at that pawnshop the entire time.

It wasn't Freihof who had taken Keira. True to his MO, Freihof had just led someone else to her. The same monster who had almost killed Keira multiple times before.

Damien Freihof might be the psycho, but in this

case, Jonathan Cunningham was just as dangerous for Keira. Roman knew he had to find her immediately or there was no telling what Cunningham would do to her.

He turned away from the women and had his phone out in an instant, calling Steve Drackett.

"Roman. You okay?"

"Freihof *was* at the pawnshop, Steve. There's no doubt about it. He drew me out there to get Keira alone."

"How could he get to Keira if he was at the pawnshop where you were?"

"He didn't come after her himself." Roman fought to keep the panic from overwhelming him. He had to focus. "He sent her ex-husband, Jonathan Cunningham, a man with a violent history against her, to take her."

He heard Steve's savage curse. It matched exactly what he felt.

"I need her tracking device activated again."

"We've got a bigger problem here at HQ. You know that text you got from me—the one I didn't send? The one that led you to the pawnshop?"

"Yeah."

"Every single active Omega agent received a similar text. Basically, the same line of information, but with a location somewhere close to them based on their GPS location."

Now it was Roman's turn to curse. Whoever

the mole was definitely knew what he or she was doing.

"So if the mole is sending out false communication, there's no reason to assume that the tracking device works at all," Steve said. "But if we can get any information from it, I will be sure to send it to you immediately."

Roman let out a harsh breath at Steve's words. This was pretty much as bad as it could get.

"I'm sorry, Roman. But as of right now, we have to assume all communication devices and computers within Omega are compromised. I can't even get in touch with most of the agents, who have been sent out to various locations based on bogus sightings of Freihof."

Roman could hear Steve saying something to one of his assistants before he came back on the line.

"I've got to go. If anything changes I will notify you immediately. But for right now, as much as I hate to say this, you're on your own."

Roman sat staring at the phone in his hands. He wanted to throw it. He wanted to punch a wall.

But neither would help. He knew he had to keep himself focused.

He looked over at Heather and Annabel. "Did Keira ever mention anything about her ex-husband? Anything at all?"

Annabel shook her head. "No, nothing helpful.

She only told us that he'd been abusive, to show us she understood what we had gone through."

Roman scrubbed a hand over his face. Where would Jonathan Cunningham have taken her? The only thing Roman could think to do was to get in touch with Bridgette Cunningham. Roman knew the woman hadn't had much contact with her son, but maybe she knew *something*.

He was pulling out his phone to get her number from information when a car came screeching into the parking lot. It pulled in sideways next to him.

Roman's eyes bugged out when he saw who was driving.

"Mother?"

"Bridgette Cunningham called me a few minutes ago and said she had heard from Jonathan for the first time in a year," Maureen said as she got out of the car, looking worriedly at Roman. "He told her that he and Keira were getting back together. That they were going to live happily-ever-after."

Roman didn't have time to go through another session of his mother's attempt to keep him away from Keira. "Damn it, I showed you what he did to her. Do you really think she would get back together with him?"

His mother actually rolled her eyes at him. "I would certainly hope she was too smart to get back together with him."

"Then why are you telling me this? Yes, Jonathan Cunningham has Keira. But I don't think happily-ever-after has anything to do with the plans he has."

"I didn't trust Keira. I thought she was using you."

"Yeah, Mother. I know." He turned away, to go inside and see if he could find any clues as to where she might have been taken. If not, Bridgette would be the next person he talked to.

"I had her followed, okay? I thought she was pulling something over on you so I had her followed, so that I would have proof of that. When I found out last week how much she really meant to you, I canceled the private investigator who was tailing her. But since I already paid through to the end of the month, the guy is still on her."

Roman spun around, barely willing to believe what he thought his mother was saying.

She nodded at him. "I know where Jonathan has taken Keira."

Chapter Twenty-Three

Riding in the car with Jonathan, her hands and feet tied, Keira struggled to keep the panic from swamping her. Next to her, Jonathan hummed along with the radio.

When she'd been married to him, he'd been violent. Now, he was evidently violent and crazy.

What Bridgette had said was true. Jonathan's mental health had definitely deteriorated over the last few years. Keira couldn't help but think that her chances would've been better with Damien Freihof.

She kept her body as far away from him as she could, and her tone as neutral as possible. "Where are we going, Jonathan?"

He stopped humming and glanced over at her. She didn't feel any more secure at the smile he gave her. "To our house, darling."

He had kept their house even all these years later? "We are going all the way to Denver?"

"Oh no, no. Mother and Father made me sell

that house. But don't worry. I had one built just like it. An exact replica."

That he'd had an exact replica of their house built just added to the panic inside her.

"Don't worry, it's not far now. I knew eventually we'd get back together and I wanted us to have privacy."

They had left Colorado Springs a few miles ago and were now on some remote country road. The farther they went, the more Keira knew she was in trouble. One of the first things Jonathan had done was throw her phone away. So Roman wouldn't be able to track her that way. If Roman hadn't walked into a trap.

"Are you working with Damien Freihof?" Like always, she never knew what question might send Jonathan into a rage, but she had to know if Roman was okay.

Jonathan gave her another friendly smile. "Damien is my friend. He helped me find you. Convinced me that you would want to spend time with me."

Keira fought to keep from cringing. How could anyone, especially Jonathan, think that she would want to spend time with him?

"Because I wanted to kill you right then," Jonathan continued, in the same conversational tone. "But Damien convinced me otherwise. Now we can live together for a while before I kill you."

Keira tamped down her terror and her anger. She didn't want to allow Jonathan to browbeat her again, but she wanted to stay alive. If there was any chance for her to get out of this she needed to play it smart. To cater to him. He'd always liked it when she was afraid.

It went against every molecule of the woman she'd become to allow herself to act terrified of Jonathan, rather than stay angry and fight him. But she would do it. She would act browbeaten and submissive.

Because she couldn't bear to think what it would do to the baby if Jonathan began beating her like he had in the past.

"I hope we can live together for a long time," she said quietly, trying not to choke on the words.

Jonathan just smiled.

They were going farther and farther down this road that seemed to lead nowhere. She worried about Roman. Had he walked into a trap? Was he okay or had Freihof gotten to him the way that Jonathan had gotten to her?

She had to believe that Roman was okay. That was the only way she could continue right now.

When the road bent around a group of trees, Keira blanched. There right in front of her, in the middle of nowhere, was an exact replica of the house she and Jonathan had lived in when they'd been married.

Jonathan looked excited. "See? I had it built. It took a lot of money." A stormy expression overtook his features. Keira knew from experience that wasn't a good sign.

"It's beautiful," she said quickly. "I'm so glad you brought me here to show it to me."

Jonathan parked the car in front of the door, then came around to Keira's side of the car. He reached down and picked her up out of the vehicle, holding her in his arms. Keira fought not to let her distaste show. She didn't want him to touch her, and she damn well didn't want him to be holding her in his arms like a groom crossing the threshold.

He opened the unlocked door and pushed his way inside. Keira grew even more distraught when she saw that the interior was just as similar to their old house as the outside was.

"You made it perfect," she whispered, hoping it sounded more intimate and not how she really felt: violently ill. "It feels just like home."

"You should've never left me, Keira." He shook his head sadly. "I'll have to punish you for that. Make you understand that a wife's place is with her husband."

Terror flooded her entire body. She knew what those quiet, calm words meant. Had heard them many times before. He set her gently on the couch.

And then backhanded her so hard she fell over.

She could taste blood in her mouth as she struggled to get her bearings.

"Why did you leave me, Keira?"

Keira used her tied hands to push herself back into a sitting position. She knew from experience that lying down just made it easier for him to punch her.

But once she sat up, she realized he had a gun and it was pointed right at her head.

"I loved you so much, Keira. And you left me. We're not supposed to live without each other. Don't you know that?"

Keira had to think fast. This Jonathan was definitely not the same man she'd been married to. The Jonathan she'd married had been alternately charming and violent.

This man was violent and homicidal. A much worse combination.

"Of course I know we are supposed to be together. I'm so glad you found me, Jonathan. I didn't want to leave you."

He at least took the gun away from her head. "You didn't? But you've been gone for so many weeks now."

Oh, dear God, he thought she'd been gone only for weeks? His mental health was obviously much more deteriorated than anybody had known.

"And they've been the longest weeks of my life." She almost choked on the words, but forced them out. "I needed to think things through. You can understand that, right?"

Jonathan nodded solemnly, his brown eyes cloudy, definitely unaware of reality.

He trailed a finger down her cheek and she barely refrained from flinching. "Yes. I do understand that. And what's important now is that you and I are here together. Finally. Our final resting place together."

Keira realized that this man was much more dangerous than the Jonathan she had known. This one was determined that they would both die. She saw him bring up the gun again.

"Jonathan, the reason I left," she said, as quickly as possible, "is because I'm pregnant. We're going to have a baby."

She closed her eyes as she said it. This lie seemed worse to her than all the others. Especially not knowing if Roman was okay. If Freihof had gotten to him.

But like always, Keira knew she had to do whatever she could to survive.

"We're having a baby?" Wonder was evident in Jonathan's tone.

She smiled. "Yes, I'm pregnant."

This obviously changed things for Jonathan. Some factor he had not considered. Keira watched silently as he paced back and forth for a long time, muttering to himself. She didn't want to interrupt him, didn't want to bring his attention back to her. She used the time to glance around as much as possible without it being evident. She had to figure a way out of here.

Because she was on her own.

Jonathan was beginning to look at her with more and more skepticism. Did he think she was lying?

She smiled at him. "Do you mind just untying my feet? My ankles have been a little swollen." She made her smile brighter. "You know, pregnancy stuff. Our baby, Jonathan."

The skepticism melted away, which was what she had been hoping for, as he bent down to look at her feet.

"I won't untie your hands," he said. "So don't even ask me. I can't trust you not to run away again, even with the baby."

She nodded. "I understand. I broke your trust. I won't do that again."

That reassured him a little bit, evidently, because he bent lower and untied the rope.

For the first time Keira had a sense of hope. Now all she had to do was get away from him. With her feet unbound, she could at least run.

She didn't let herself think too hard about the state of the weather outside. It wasn't a blizzard, but it was still February in Colorado. She wouldn't last long if she didn't find help.

But she would last longer than she would against Jonathan and his gun if he changed his mind about how he felt about the baby, or realized how long she'd really been gone and that if she was pregnant, the baby couldn't possibly be his.

Unfortunately, that moment came sooner rather than later.

They'd probably been at the house a total of thirty or forty minutes. Keira wasn't sure what triggered the clarity in Jonathan, but when he turned to her she saw that he had a clear grip on reality.

"Keira?" He looked at her as if he was seeing her for the first time today. Which perhaps he was. "How did you get here?"

She looked into his eyes, which were clear for the first time. "You brought me here, remember?"

His eyes narrowed at her words and he glanced around, obviously trying to remember what had happened over the last hour. Finally, he looked back at her.

"You're pregnant?"

Keira got up and ran. She didn't wait to see how long it would take for him to figure out exactly what was going on. She just knew *this* was the man who had hurt her so many times. He would kill her now that he knew she was pregnant with another man's child.

He caught her before she even reached the front

door, grabbing her by her hair and yanking her back onto the floor. Keira let out a sob.

"Pregnant?" His hot breath was right next to her ear, causing her to shudder. "That baby's not mine and we both know it."

He kept hold of her hair as he dragged her into the bedroom. Keira began sobbing. She couldn't bear it if he actually touched her.

But he didn't drag her to the bed. Instead he pulled her to a wooden chair in the middle of the room—the only thing that didn't match the furnishings from their first house. He took out some rope and wrapped it around her chest, securing her to the chair. Then he did the same with her ankles.

"Did you think I built this place because I wanted to have the great memories of our time together?" He spat the words at her. "Don't flatter yourself."

This was the Jonathan she had known. Full of rage and self-righteousness.

"After you left me, my parents cut me off. I had to steal money from them to build this house," he continued. "I wanted to make sure I had this so when I found you again, I could make sure you burned without me getting caught."

When he finished tying her he came and stood right in front of her, his face merely inches from her own.

"I'm going to do in this house what I should've

done in our first one. Kill you, you ungrateful bitch. You're going to burn to ash right here in our happy home."

"Jonathan—"

He struck her again, snapping her head to the side. "I would gag you, but I want to hear you scream as you die."

He walked over to the closet and pulled out a large canister of gasoline and began dousing the far side of the room.

"I won't pour gasoline on you. I want to make sure you suffer as long as possible. You and your baby." His face turned a mottled red as he said it. "You deserve everything coming to you."

He turned and walked toward the bedroom door, glancing back over his shoulder right before he left.

"You know what's great about all of this? Even if someone does find your body, which is unlikely, let's be honest, everyone will blame Damien Freihof. It's not every day you find someone willing to take the credit for your murders. I'll get off scot-free."

He gave her one more rage-filled smile, lit a match, threw it on the floor and walked out.

Chapter Twenty-Four

The private investigator had been paid only to see where Keira went, and keep a record. So once he knew where the house was, the man had left.

As much as Roman wished he had someone who could rush in right then to help Keira, he was at least thankful he had an address. As soon as he knew the location, about twenty miles outside town, he was on his way.

He was less than an hour behind them, but terror gripped him at the thought of what could happen to Keira in an hour at Jonathan Cunningham's hands.

Roman knew he needed a plan, but there were too many unknowns to even come up with one. All he knew was that he had to get to Keira as fast as possible. His mother had wanted to come with him, to help, but Roman hadn't even listened to her. What he needed now were his SWAT teammates, but none of his calls had gone through.

Roman had no doubt that was due to the work of the traitor inside Omega.

Roman was on his own.

He found the house easily enough, but parked his truck about a quarter mile from it for stealth. He didn't want Cunningham to kill Keira as soon as he saw Roman. He grabbed his sidearm and sprinted the rest of the way, praying all the while that he was not too late.

The house was completely out of place in the middle of the woods. It looked like something that belonged in a suburban neighborhood.

And Jonathan Cunningham was standing in front of it, laughing.

"Cunningham, get your hands up where I can see them," Roman said as he closed in on him. At least if he was out here he wasn't harming Keira.

"So much for a secret location," the man muttered under his breath.

"Where is Keira?"

"Are you him?"

Roman pointed his weapon more fully at Cunningham. "Where is Keira?" he asked again.

"You're him, aren't you? The father of her baby." Cunningham began to laugh again. "Well, not for long."

It was then that Roman smelled the smoke. The house was on fire, and obviously Cunningham had trapped Keira in there. He called 911, curs-

ing when the call wouldn't go through because of
whatever the mole had done.

Roman made a dash for the door. He didn't care
if the building was already burning; he was not
leaving Keira in there.

But before he could make it, Cunningham's
weight crashed into him and sent them both flying into the dirt next to the door.

Roman's gun went flying out of his hand back
behind them.

"No. She's going to burn in there the way she
should've burned a long time ago."

Roman felt Cunningham's fist connect with his
jaw, the force knocking his head to the side. But
Roman refused to allow the blow to stun him. He
shifted his weight, rolling forward so that he was
on top. This time, it was his fist that flew into
Cunningham's face.

Roman didn't even try to filter the sense of
joy he received from feeling Cunningham's nose
break under his knuckles. The other man howled.

Roman grabbed him up by his collar, remem-
bering how Cunningham had broken Keira's nose.
"Doesn't feel so great, does it?"

Roman slammed the man back down and ran
toward the house. More smoke barreled out now.

"Keira!"

Again, Cunningham's weight crashed into him.

Roman didn't have time to fight the other man. Every second he remained out here was a second Keira stayed trapped in the burning building. Roman threw his elbow up to connect with the other man's face, but still Cunningham held on.

They both knew he wouldn't win in a fight against Roman. But Cunningham didn't have to win, he just had to stall Roman until it would be too late to save Keira.

Cunningham wrapped his arms around Roman in a bear hug. "She's going to die. You may kill me, but I'm going to make sure she dies today."

Roman threw all his weight backward, breaking free. He turned and hit the man with a solid uppercut to the jaw. Cunningham fell to the ground, unconscious.

Fire was escaping the windows now. Roman ran to the door and kicked it in, but was knocked backward by the force of the flames that rushed out as they gained more oxygen.

There was no way anyone could be alive in that living room. Roman would have to make his way around to the back and hope he could get in there, that the back of the house was burning more slowly than the front. He refused to accept that Keira was gone.

Roman began sprinting around the house but stopped when Cunningham stood up.

And pointed his gun straight at Roman.

Roman's weapon was still lying near the side of the house, where it had been knocked from his hands.

"You're too late. She's already dead. I made sure she burned."

Roman glanced over at the house. Smoke was billowing from every possible window now. There was no way someone could survive inside. Devastation ate through everything in his body.

"But don't worry," Cunningham continued. "You'll soon be joining her. And honestly, I'll be surprised if they find your bodies in the next year."

A rage filled Roman. If this son of a bitch had killed Keira, Roman wasn't going to just stand here and allow Cunningham to shoot him. If he was going to die, he was going to die fighting.

He dived for Cunningham and heard the gun fire twice. He braced himself for the pain as he piled into the man, knocking them both to the ground.

But the pain never came.

It took Roman only a moment to realize that Cunningham wasn't moving. Wasn't fighting him at all. Roman jumped to his feet, his only thought to get to Keira, still in the building, in case a miracle had happened.

And found the miracle standing five yards in front of him.

Keira stood, with the support of his mother, holding Roman's gun.

Cunningham wasn't fighting because Keira had shot him.

Barely able to believe his eyes, Roman staggered over to the two women.

"What? How?" he asked as he wrapped Keira in his arms.

"I followed you," Maureen said, straightening her blouse as if she hadn't just run into a burning building. "While you were fighting I went around the back and got Keira out."

"Thank you, Maureen," Keira said, her voice scratchy from smoke inhalation.

Maureen just shrugged. "I was wrong about too many things when it came to you, Keira. I might have brought Jonathan back into your life by meddling with Bridgette. I'm glad I could at least make this right, although let's not do this again. I don't think I'm cut out for this SWAT stuff, Roman."

"Mom…" Roman didn't even know how to get the words out. His mother had just risked her own life and saved his entire future. There was no way Roman could've gotten into that building in time to save Keira and the baby. "I…"

Maureen touched him on the shoulder, nodding. "I know, son." She smiled at both of them. "Besides, I couldn't let anything happen to my grandbaby."

Roman and Keira laughed, and both held out an arm to pull Maureen into the hug with them.

Freihof and the mole were still out there, still critical for Omega. They had to be stopped, and they would be. But right now, Roman was just happy knowing Keira and the baby were safe.

Chapter Twenty-Five

Two Months Later

Keira sat on the couch looking at what used to be the wall of the apartment connected to hers. Now it was all one larger apartment, effectively making her one-bedroom unit into a three-bedroom.

Once Roman and Maureen had gotten Keira's approval, they'd brought someone in to do the work very quickly. Maureen was in the salon daily, talking about paint chips and textures for floors and bathroom tiles. Evidently, whatever effort his mother had once put into keeping Keira out of Roman's life was now being put into decorating their new home.

"Freaking out?" Roman asked, as he came and sat next to her on the couch, handing her a cup of hot green tea.

She glanced sideways at him. "Your mom is a little scary."

Roman laughed. "Yeah, once she decides to put

her energy toward something, she goes at it full force. If it helps, I think she's still trying to make up for her error in judgment before."

"She was trying to protect you. I didn't like it, but I can understand what she was trying to do."

"Is she getting too involved here? I can have her back off. I'm used to her ways, but I'm sure it can be a little overwhelming."

He slipped an arm around Keira and she slid closer to his side. This was how they had spent most evenings since the day Jonathan had kidnapped her. The next day Roman had shown up at her apartment with most of his clothes and toiletries, and basically had never left.

Not that Keira wanted him to.

"No, I think that Annabel and Heather like having her around. And I don't think your mom would be able to give up her time with little Rachel even if I told her she had to stop the decorating."

Maureen had formed a special bond with Heather and her daughter. The older woman often came in now to hold the baby while Heather was working.

"Yeah, training for when our baby gets here."

Keira turned so she could face him directly. "Are you sure about living here? I know even with the new apartment added we're not going to have a whole lot of space. Definitely not as much as a big house."

"Why would I need a big house? Everything I want is right here." His hand slid to cover her belly, which was starting to show signs of the growing life inside her.

"But what about when you decide to do stuff politically? An apartment over a salon…is it really going to work for that?"

"Who says I'm planning to go into politics?"

Keira rolled her eyes. "Um, let me see. You. Your mother. Anybody who knows you. Anybody who knew your father."

"Dad wanted to help. That's why he ran for state senate. And he was great at it."

Keira shrugged. "You might be great at it, too."

"I want to help. I want to make a difference. But that doesn't necessarily mean running for office. I can make a difference from right here. From Fresh Starts. Put my time and effort and financial resources into shelters like this and other ones all across the country."

A weight lifted. "You're sure? I don't want to hold you back from something that's important to you."

"Making a difference is important to me. But you and the baby are important to me, too." His large hands reached up and framed her face and pulled her in for a kiss. She was breathless by the time they were done.

"Okay?" he said against her mouth.

She nodded. Then relaxed as he eased her back into his side.

"I want you to marry me," he said, after a long moment.

Keira hated that she couldn't stop herself from stiffening at the word. She knew Roman wasn't Jonathan. Knew the Weber family weren't the Cunninghams.

"Roman…" She didn't want to say anything that would damage their relationship, but didn't know if she would ever be able to say yes to a marriage proposal. She tried to get up from the couch, but he wouldn't let her.

"Keira, look at me."

She didn't want to, but she did.

"Do you love me?"

Yes. Yes, she did love him. She knew that. But loving him and convincing her mind that it was okay to get married again? Those were two very different things.

"Yes." She whispered softly, afraid everything was about to fall apart. "I do love you, Roman. I hope you believe that."

He smiled. "I do believe it. And I love you, too. I think I've been in love with you from that first night at Brandon and Andrea's wedding."

How was she going to be able to explain to him that she felt the same way, but that the thought of marriage terrified her? That her fear of tying herself to him legally had nothing to do with lack of feelings for him?

How could she ever make him understand something like that?

Roman reached over to the table beside the couch and grabbed an envelope and a ring box.

Oh God, a ring box.

Keira was afraid she was going to start sobbing at any second.

"Roman…"

He held the envelope and the box up between them. "This is for when you're ready. I know you're not ready right now, and that's okay.

"This is a prenuptial agreement," he continued. "Different than what would normally be in a prenuptial agreement. Our family lawyer had a fit."

Keira took it, since Roman obviously wanted her to.

"It was my mother's idea, actually," he said.

That stung a little bit, after how things had changed between her and Maureen, but Keira wasn't surprised.

"Maureen wants to protect her family—don't blame her for that. I don't."

Roman smiled. "Yes, she does want to protect her family. But that now includes you and the baby."

Keira's brows furrowed. She opened the envelope. She wasn't any legal expert, but she could tell right away that he'd been correct when he'd stated this wasn't a normal prenuptial agreement. "I'm not sure I understand exactly what this says. It can't mean what I think it does."

"Well, let me use my law degree to explain it to you. Basically, it says that everything I own, all my inheritance and holdings within the Weber family, are all given to you and the baby once we're married."

"What? Why?"

"It means that you never have to worry about being in a position of helplessness ever again within a marriage. That everything I have is yours." He ran a finger down her cheek. "That's true even without a piece of paper. But my mother thought it might make you feel more at ease, given what happened in your previous marriage."

Keira wasn't sure exactly what to say. That they would understand, that they would go to such lengths to make her feel secure… She just dipped her head until it rested against Roman's chest.

"I'm a little embarrassed to say it," he continued, rubbing gentle circles on her back. "But the ring was my mother's idea, too. It was hers when she was married to my father. I want you to have it. *She* wants you to have it."

When Keira looked up at him again, his face was blurry because of her tears.

"For when you're ready, Keira." He caught a tear with his finger as it trailed down her cheek. "And if you're never ready, that's okay, too. Because either way, there's nowhere else I'm going. No place I'd rather be than right here with you and our baby and our babies to come."

She nodded. "I will marry you, Roman. As soon as I possibly can, as soon as I am possibly able, I will marry you. But I have to tell you, I don't know when that will be."

She felt him slip the ring on her finger.

"Then we'll discover it together. And it will be worth the wait."

* * * * *

Don't miss the next book in Janie Crouch's
OMEGA SECTOR: UNDER SIEGE
miniseries: MAJOR CRIMES

And look for the previous books in the
OMEGA SECTOR: UNDER SIEGE *series:*
DADDY DEFENDER
PROTECTOR'S INSTINCT

Available now wherever
Harlequin Intrigue books are sold!